CRUSTACEANS

BY

WILLIAM MEIKLE

SEVEREDPRESS

CRUSTACEANS

Copyright © 2024 WILLIAM MEIKLE

WWW.SEVEREDPRESS.COM

All rights reserved. No part of this book may be reproduced or transmitted in any form or by any electronic or mechanical means, including photocopying, recording or by any information and retrieval system, without the written permission of the publisher and author, except where permitted by law.
This novel is a work of fiction. Names, characters, places and incidents are the product of the author's imagination, or are used fictitiously. Any resemblance to actual events, locales or persons, living or dead, is purely coincidental.

ISBN: 978-1-923165-31-1

1

The whale farted.

The noise was like a cotton sheet being slowly ripped in two. The body shuddered along its whole length in a long slow ripple. The three men standing beside it giggled nervously, then had to stand back as the odour tickled their nostrils.

"Are you *sure* it's dead?" Toms asked, pinching fingers to his nose and breathing as lightly as he could through his mouth.

"Just intestinal gases finding their way out," McGuire said. "Nothing to worry about."

"That smell isn't *just* anything," Toms replied. "It's so thick I can chew it."

He sniffed at his clothes. "And it's sinking into my jacket. I do believe it's toxic."

McGuire nodded.

"Sure is ripe. And that's just the first of many."

As if to accentuate his point the whale farted again. McGuire had to turn his head away, and it was several seconds before he could speak.

"Let's get the blood and tissue samples. Then we'll call it a night. This big boy isn't going anywhere. Maybe in the morning the gases will have worked their way out."

"Or maybe the wind will get up and keep it from hanging around too long," Toms said. "But whatever you say boss. One tissue sample, coming up."

The dead sperm whale was laid out along the beach just above the water line. It had been found that same morning by a dog walker. McGuire took the call just after lunch, and they were on site less than an hour later. The whale was already dead, and from the looks of it, it had been for a few days at least. Earlier there had been a large crowd of gawpers, and even a crew from a local television station, but a dead whale doesn't do much except lie there and rot. The crowd grew bored and dissipated as dusk started to fall. Not so the small group of researchers. For them this was a big deal.

The stretch of sea around Nantucket is full of whales, but normally they are the people-pleasers… lively playful humpbacks and bottlenose dolphins that can be guaranteed to put on a show for the tourists. Sperm whales are much more sedate. They do little more than lie on the surface like huge inflated inner tubes, occasionally sending out a huge blow, and are usually only seen in deep water. Every year they trawl up and down the Eastern Seaboard, but many miles offshore. To get this close, even if it was dead, was a big thrill for the members of the team.

"What do you think is the cause of death?" Kaminski said. He was the youngest of the three, and by far the most excited. He couldn't keep his hands off the whale, and kept running his palm across the broad belly, as if it was a sleeping pet.

McGuire shrugged.

"We won't know that until we get the lab results back. And we won't get them unless we take the samples. Come on guys, focus here. Let's get the job done and head off for a few beers."

"Sounds good to me boss," Toms replied. He took a long bore from the field kit and placed it against the whale's belly.

"I'd stand well back," he said. "The last one of these I did was messy."

He started to turn the bore, twisting the overlarge corkscrew into the whale. The skin started to split in a wound that rapidly widened showing a pink layer of blubber beneath. Toms made one more turn. The belly burst open, covering the men in a flood of blood and gore.

"Shit," Toms said, and spat out a solid chunk. "It tastes even worse than it smells."

Kaminski laughed out loud.

"I guess we'll be doing the laundry before going for a beer guys."

Clickety-click.

McGuire heard the sound, but had been blinded by the spray of blood in his eyes. He reached up with his right hand to wipe it away.

Snick.

A lancing pain, white hot, shot up his arm. He reached for his eyes again. His arm never made it. His hand was no longer where it was supposed to be. Confused, he waved his arm in front of his face. Hot blood washed over him and into his mouth. He gagged and spat.

Snickety-snick.

He felt a new pain at the same time as his left leg gave way under him. He fell to the sand.

What the hell is going on?

Somewhere Toms and Kaminski screamed… high wails of terror. McGuire put his left hand on the ground, trying to push himself upright. Something grabbed him tight around the waist. It didn't feel like a friendly hug.

Snick.

The whole lower half of McGuire's body suddenly came loose, like the mother and father of all bowel movements.

He felt no pain as darkness seeped in around his thoughts.

All fell silent.

Toms and Kaminski were no longer screaming. The only sound McGuire heard was the one he struggled to identify at the end.

Clickety-clack. Clickety-clack.

2

The morning found Joe Porter out on Bellport Bay in his boat, trying to clear his head after a slew of booze the night before. Early sunlight danced on the water and lanced into his brain like tiny needles, each one bringing a stinging reminder of his excesses.

The hangover was nothing new. Joe and the bottle were old friends. His father introduced them, back on Joe's fourteenth birthday. It was the closest relationship of Joe's life, if not the most rewarding. They had been getting closer than ever over the past two years which, not entirely coincidentally, were Joe's forty-eighth and forty-ninth on the planet.

Fifty fucking years on this here Bay. And what have I got to show for it? A cabin that'll fall down in the next high wind and a stripper who'll fuck off as soon as somebody better comes along. What a fucking life.

He reached for his hip pocket and took out the flask that nestled there. The metal was worn and buckled into a perfect fit that cuddled at his butt-cheeks. The rye tasted warm but Joe paid that no never-mind and poured a cupful down his throat. His stomach roiled but he kept everything down. Within seconds the booze started running around in his bloodstream and Joe began to feel the buzz that was going to make the rest of the day at least bearable. The hangover still pounded just behind his eyes but he was thankful for it. It was one of the few things that reminded him he was alive. If he ever stopped having a thumping headache in the mornings he'd know he was in trouble.

He took another hit of rye then put the flask away.

Can't get too loaded too early. I'm not that much of a fuck-up.

The words were there in his head unbidden.

Not yet.

He pushed it away. He knew from long experience that dwelling too much on how shitty his day-to-day life had become was a sure-fire recipe for falling back into the booze. It might be good to have at least *one* sober hour today.

Besides, it was hunting season out on the Bay, and he needed to make the most of it if he was to make enough money to keep him in booze and smokes over winter. He let the boat drift twenty yards down the shore to where trees overhung the banks. There was a long mud bank here where the beasts congregated to escape the heat of the day, and it always proved a good spot to start crabbing. He cut up an eel and put out six lines, letting the fine gut hang loosely in his hand. The boat bobbed in the slight swell but didn't move enough for him to need an anchor. He sat back against the gunwale and let the sea relax him. Another slug from the hip flask and a cigarette helped him on the way a bit further.

He saw several other boats drift into position along the bank. Sometimes they would get together and share a quart or two, but Porter didn't feel like company today.

The morning drifted on. He managed to keep the hip flask in his pocket, but was running out of smokes, and none of the lines had so much as twitched. You got days like this out on the water... days that would drive a man to drink… if he wasn't already there.

He was just thinking that he might give up and get the serious drinking started when he felt a tug on one of his lines. Slowly, carefully, he brought up the first Blue Crab of the day. It wriggled in his hand but didn't have the strength in its claws to do him any serious damage. He placed it in the net in the bottom of the boat and watched it scuttle for a while.

It was the first of many. It proved to be the most successful morning's fishing he'd ever had. It was as if the crabs were being *herded* towards him. All he had to do was throw lines overboard and the crabs were onto them immediately. Within an hour his net was full and bulging. Fifty yards away Stu Watts gave him a thumbs-up as he too pulled in line after line.

Porter waved back, then swore as he felt a claw close on his thumb. A crab swung from the digit, holding tight.

"Fucker!" he shouted and tossed the offending crab into the bottom of the boat. It scuttled back towards him. He kicked it away while sucking at the welt it had raised. It hadn't quite broken the skin but it would be bruised later. The crab came back again. He raised a foot, intending to put an end to it once and for all.

It was only then that he noticed the size of the crab.

That sure as hell ain't no Blue Crab.

It was half again as big as anything else he'd ever caught in the Bay. It was grey-blue along the shell, pink below, and shining white at the claws. Its mandibles looked huge in proportion as it waved them in the air, as if tasting Porter's scent.

Clickity-clack.

It snapped a claw at him, as if warning him not to try anything.

Sparky little bugger, ain't you?

It came forward again, snapping. Porter lifted his feet out of the way, but even then it tried to snip at his heels. He grabbed the crab and stuffed it in the net. It immediately started attacking the Blue Crabs, claws snicking away legs and cutting through shell. The Blues tried to fight back but the newcomer was stronger, bigger and altogether way more vicious. Porter sat there watching his earnings getting butchered.

It's almost as if the fucker is enjoying it.

He made for shore, the joy gone from the morning.

On the way back he finished off the contents of the hip-flask. He had a good buzz on by the time he moored the boat, and wasn't quite co-ordinated as he made his way back along the dock.

He made a hash of emptying the net. Bits of Blue Crab fell with a clatter, some of the pieces dropping with a splash through the boards. The large crab landed on its back but righted itself quickly and made a bid for freedom, scuttling across the small deck at the front of the cabin.

Porter caught it just before it reached the water. He was careful this time; approaching it from behind and making sure the pincers were kept well away from his fingers. The crab *snapped* furiously. Porter lifted the crab in front of him and looked straight at it. It stared back from small white, unblinking eyes. Porter smiled, and spat on it.

You're mine now fucker. Better start getting used to it.

He took it indoors, sealing it in a large empty fish-tank he'd bought for setting up an aquarium but never got round to using. As soon as he closed the lid the crab banged angrily on the glass with its claws. It scuttled around the four sides of the tank, smacking on the glass all the way.

It's looking for a weak point.

"Noisy little fucker, aren't you?" Porter said.

It stopped banging and stared at him again. For the first time Porter had a really close look at it. It had eight red legs. It stood on *tip-toe* on all of them, pincers raised above its head, like a martial arts expert waiting to strike, its body partially angled towards him so that he could see its belly and what looked *remarkably* like a face. It looked at Porter, then banged hard on the glass right in front of his nose, causing him to flinch and step back. Even when he went outside and started to pack what was left of the Blue Crab catch in ice for transportation, he heard the *knock-knock* of the claws on the glass.

Once he was finished packing the catch he went back inside, broke open the rum and sat in his chair studying the large crab. As he'd originally thought, it was the biggest he'd ever caught in the Bay, by some way. And there was something about this one that chilled his blood.

I should kill it and be done with it. It might even make good eating.

But it was a curio, something new in the routine of his day to day existence, and as such it needed to be cherished, if only for a short time.

"Enjoy your new home fucker," he whispered to it. "I'll be keeping you for a while longer. Let's see what you grow into."

The crab knocked angrily against the glass while Porter made a dive into the rum.

3

Shona Menzies sat alone in the spacious rear passenger seat of a sleek black Hummer and wondered where they were taking her.

They were far away from any roads she recognised and from where she sat she couldn't see any of the direction signs on the highway. Even when she *did* finally catch a glimpse of one the vehicle was moving too fast for her to read it. For maybe the tenth time she thought about asking the men up front where they were heading, but she knew she'd get the same answer.

That's classified Miss. I'm sure they'll fill you in when we get there.

She was worried.

Who wouldn't be?

She'd been roused out of bed at two in the morning and opened the door to find two bulky armed men.

"*Homeland Security,*" they had said. "Please come with us Ms Menzies."

"If it's my visa, I have another two months left," she said.

"It's not your visa Miss. Please come with us. We don't have much time if we're to get you there by morning."

"Get me where?"

"Sorry Miss, that's classified."

She'd only been given time to get dressed and throw as much as she could into a travelling bag then they bundled her into the Hummer. They'd been driving south for hours now, and she was no nearer an explanation.

They overtook a truck whose driver gave them a long angry *hoot* as they cut in front of him.

"What's the hurry?" she asked.

"We were told to get you ASAP," the one in the passenger seat said. "And when the Colonel says ASAP, he means *yesterday.*"

"I'm not that important," she replied.

"If the Colonel says…" he started.

She interrupted him.

"Yes, I get *that* picture. Look, are you *sure* you've got the right person?" she asked, but she just got the same blank stare as before. Both men were big-built and hefty, with close-cut blonde hair. Both wore dark casual jackets over black shirts and either one was as quiet as the other was.

"Do you two even have names? Or did they clone you?" she asked.

That *did* get a smile from the man in the passenger seat up front.

"I'm Lieutenant John Wilkes," he said and turned to look at her. He had piercing blue eyes and a white scar running down the left side of his face, but the smile looked genuine enough, and did something, just a little, to dispel some of Shona's unease.

Wilkes continued.

"And your driver tonight is Sergeant Matthews."

Matthews grunted in reply.

"Don't mind him Miss," Wilkes said. "I got him out of bed just before we came for you."

She looked from one to the other. There was no sign of insignia, no evidence they were in fact who they said they were.

Just because you're paranoid doesn't mean they're not out to get you.

"So which one of you do I have to sleep with to get a coffee?"

Wilkes smiled broadly.

"That would be me. The Sergeant here is a married man," he said. He reached down to a panel between the seats and brought out a thermos. "But we don't have time right now. Can I take a rain check?"

She smiled back. She was actually starting to relax.

And I've got them talking. Well, one of them at least.

"Which force are you with? Where are you taking me?"

"Coffee for sex, that was the deal, right?" Wilkes said with a smile. "You never said anything about classified information. That would cost you a lot more."

Once again they went back to the blank stares as they drove through the darkness.

The coffee was good though, strong and black, giving her body the jolt it needed to keep her going for a while longer. They slowed down at a junction and, for the first time, she saw a sign.

Boston? What are we doing in fucking Boston?

She hadn't realised she'd spoken aloud.

Wilkes turned and smiled again.

"Don't worry Miss. We're just passing through."

Through to where?

By the time they pulled up on a sandy shoreline she was close to screaming in frustration.

"Please stay put," Wilkes said. "Just for a minute longer."

The two men got out. Just as Shona reached for the door the locks closed with a loud click.

This time she *did* scream, but it didn't get her anywhere. Nobody paid her any attention. She saw black clad men outside the Hummer, all of whom seemed busy with something.

It was another five minutes before they finally let her out.

"Okay," Wilkes said as he opened the door for her. "End of the road."

"Now do I get told what the hell is going on?" she said.

A tall dark haired man walked towards her and thrust out a hand to be shaken.

He at least looks military.

She couldn't have taken him for anything else. He looked to be in his late thirties, maybe a year or two either side of forty. He carried himself stiff and straight, he didn't have a hair out of place and, although he wore a black sweatshirt and black pants, he wore it as if it was a uniform. She expected a clipped, stern voice to go with the look and was surprised by a soft Southern drawl that was almost whispered.

"Colonel Stack," he said. "I'm sorry for the inconvenience, but we needed to get you here in a hurry. I trust they looked after you?"

She laughed.

"Oh yes. We had a *wonderful* trip, full of witty conversation and giddy delights."

She saw immediately that Stark's sarcasm detector was not a well-developed part of his armoury; he looked puzzled by her remark. She decided to plough on regardless.

"So what *exactly* does *Homeland Security* need with a marine biologist?"

He smiled, but there was a strain in his eyes that told her he hadn't slept for a while.

"We were told you were the expert on this kind of thing."

She sighed loudly.

"For *fucks* sake, just tell me. I've had enough of this cloak and dagger shit."

Wilkes looked ready to laugh, but a glance from the Colonel quickly put paid to that.

"Whatever you want Miss Menzies," he said, and pronounced the name the Scottish way.

He is full of surprises this one.

Stark led her round the side of the Hummer and for the first time she got sight of the carcass of the whale that lay there.

She smiled.

"I *knew* there had been a mistake. I deal in *crustaceans* not *cetaceans*."

"No mistake Miss," Stack said. He took her by the arm. His grip was firm, but not painful, as he led her over to the whale. Or, more precisely, what was left of it.

My God. It exploded.

That was her first thought. She'd seen bloated carcasses before, in situations where the vegetable material in the dead beast's stomach started to ferment in hot damp conditions. At first glance this looked to be the case here. The whole belly had been laid open.

But when she looked closer she saw that this hadn't been a standard case of spontaneous bloating. Something had hacked its way out. The sand for yards around was red and damp. The air smelled, heavy with the tang of blood and stomach acid. She put her hand across her mouth and stepped in closer. The edges of the flesh were not ragged. Indeed they looked cleanly snipped, as if by scissors.

Or claws?

Something shifted in the pit of her stomach, a sinking feeling as she had the first inclination of why she'd been rudely awakened.

She turned to Stark.

"What happened here?" she asked. "You didn't bring me all this way in the middle of the night to look at a dead whale."

"No Miss Menzies. We didn't."

Stark led her towards the far side of the whale. Two field tents were set up on the shore above the beach. An ambulance was parked at the side, doors closed. A pale-faced medic stood to one side, smoking a cigarette, looking drawn and shaky. Stark led her into the nearest tent.

"Three researchers were working on the whale," he said, and paused, as if wondering how much to tell her. "They were *butchered*… there's no other word for it. We found pieces of them all over the beach. It was like a war zone. We've only just got through cleaning up."

The worry grew bigger in her.

"How does this involve *Homeland Security*," she asked. She was buying time, hoping against hope that her suspicions would be proved wrong.

"I was called in a couple of weeks back when it was obvious *something* was happening."

He sat her down next to a laptop.

"This was taken off the coast of Cuba, two months ago," he said, and accessed a menu. The laptop's DVD drive whirred into action.

The screen showed an underwater scene. At first it looked completely out of focus, but someone behind the camera sharpened it up and zoomed in close on the action. Two divers in full wet suits and scuba gear approached a wreck. Twin funnels rose over rusted bows. To Shona's untrained eye it looked like a cargo boat of some kind, and one that had been sunk for some years… long enough for the corals to start encrusting it.

The divers moved slowly and carefully up to the nearest part of the rotting hull. The area was heavily silted up and their flippers disturbed whorls of sediment with each stroke. One of the divers got in front and started to try to clear an area around a hatchway. He worked on it for some time, brushing away sand. The operator took the opportunity to pan the camera around. The view showed the full length of the hulk, including a large hole halfway along lined with buckled metal that looked like it had been blown out from the inside.

By the time they panned back to the hatchway the diver had cleared the area. He reached out and turned the handle, having to use two hands and put all his strength into it. The hatchway opened slowly, revealing deep darkness inside.

The diver turned and made a circle with forefinger and thumb towards the camera. Just as he turned back something long and white *lunged* forward out of the hatchway.

The camera spun wildly.

Sediment got kicked up, obscuring the view. Things went dull and murky, making it hard to tell what was going on. White showed again, moving quickly in the murk. More sand got kicked up. Something passed in front of the camera, a white blur. Little detail was visible, but Shona saw enough to bring her worst fears rushing in.

It can't be.

The camera drifted, unmanned, to the deck and lay at an acute angle. At the far end of the deck there was a last flash of white, then all went quiet.

The swirling sand settled slowly.

A severed leg, blood oozing behind it, floated past the lens.

All went black.

Shona remembered to breathe.

"Who took the film?" she whispered.

"They were Navy Seals," Stack said. "In Cuban waters on a mission. We lost two men, and a third is still in hospital. He's missing an arm, taken clean off at the elbow, as if hit with a sword."

What killed them?

Shona didn't vocalise the question. She had a sickening feeling that she already knew the answer.

"I'm starting to see why you need me," she said, little more than a whisper.

Stark nodded.

"We needed the best. We have a serious problem."

He tapped another item on the menu.

"Florida, last month."

It was a newspaper article.

"Great White in Miami waters?"

"Local doctor Sam Johnson made a gruesome discovery this morning while taking his morning constitutional. His dog Rex brought him an unexpected gift… a shoe, with a severed human foot still inside.

"A few yards further along the shore the doctor discovered the partially digested remains of a human torso. Officials have now sealed off the beach and have reported several other body parts as being found strewn over a large area.

"Meanwhile concern is growing as to the fate of the Robbins family. The family's yacht went missing three days ago in calm seas. Rumour is spreading all along the coast of a Great White being seen cruising the area. But so far, there have been no confirmed sightings."

"It wasn't a Great White, was it?" Shona whispered.

"No. It wasn't," Stark said. "We have the autopsy report for you on the body parts that were found, and the results of a full forensic examination of the area."

"Was it the same thing as in Cuba?"

Stack didn't reply. He hit another menu item.

"This is from just last week," he said. "A young family were on the beach in Cape Charles in Virginia."

Shona heard children laughing as she turned back to the screen.

It was a home video. Two young children waved excitedly at the camera, both less than five years old.

"Chase us Daddy," one said. She took the hand of her sister and together they ran off down the beach towards the water. The person holding the camera followed slowly behind, the picture shaking and wavering in time with their steps. The kids leapt into the sea, splashing each other excitedly. The older of the two ducked the other's head under the water, bringing squeals of excitement and outrage. More water got thrown and the squeals got louder.

"Play nice kids," a voice said on camera.

The kids kept splashing, getting increasingly excited.

Shona realised she *really* did not want to see what was coming, but she couldn't keep her eyes off the screen.

"Come on Daddy," the eldest shouted. "This is *fun*."

The sea was white with splashing from flailing arms and legs.

The person carrying the camera started to move closer to the water. There was a flash of white under the water, heading towards the girls.

"Emma. Kate. Get out of there. Right now!"

The girls either didn't hear or pretended not to. They kept splashing.

There was another flash of white.

The water turned red. The splashing got frantic, spray rising high, obscuring the view of what was happening. One of the girls screamed, but the noise was quickly silenced. The camera dropped to the sand, showing only a man running to where a red slick lay on the water.

"Emma! Kate!"

His shouts turned to wails of grief.

The only other noise was a loud *clickety-clack*, like distant castanets.

Shona turned away, tears forming.

The poor babies. That poor man.

"There's one more," Stark said, leaning forward, but Shona had already seen more than enough.

They're back. Just like he said they'd be.

"Do you have a cell-phone?" she said.

"You'll find one in the Hummer," he replied.

She rose, knocking over the seat behind her, and left the tent.

"Where are you going?" Stack called after her.

"To talk to the one Menzies who *should* be here," she replied. "I need to call my father."

4

Porter kept a close eye on the crab. It was rapidly outgrowing the tank, having more than trebled in size in the two weeks since he'd caught it. It was now nearly two feet wide across the back, with a span of over three feet from claw-tip to claw-tip.

It ate ferociously, consuming everything that was put in the tank, whether it was animal or vegetable. It had a particular liking for wiener sausages that Porter found faintly nauseating. Everything went into the maw, and only little neat piles of scat came out the other end. The cage was starting to smell but Porter was wary of trying to clean it. He suspected that if he put an arm into the tank, some, maybe most, of it would be gone in seconds.

The crab looked very angry.

It banged on the glass of the aquarium, morning, noon and night. Sometimes Porter thought he could hear a rhythm in it, a manic drummer trying to send a signal. At other times he found himself joining in, fingers beating out rhythms on the arms of his chair.

The noise was driving Sarah to distraction.

"Can't you shut the little fucker up?" she asked, at least three times a day.

Then again, the girl was easily distracted. Shiny objects, crap television shows and food could all stop the flow of her thoughts almost instantly. Porter reckoned she only had three brain cells working at any one time, and even then one of them rarely spoke to the others. She was just about the dimmest creature he'd ever met. For a while she had made up for it by being spectacular in the sack, but the constant banality was wearing him down and he guessed it wouldn't be too long now before he asked her to hit the road.

The crab banged on the glass.

"Can't you shut the little fucker up?" she whined.

"Just open the lid and shake your ass at him," Porter said. "That'll give him something else to think about. And one of them claws might give you an unexpected thrill at the same time."

Porter laughed loudly as the girl gave him the finger.

"I don't know why I put up with your shit," she said petulantly.

"It must be my good looks and charm, doll," he said and leered.

She ignored him. She gingerly lifted the lid and dropped in a thick chunk of baloney. The crab scuttled over it almost before it hit the floor of the tank. It tore neat little strips from the meat and delivered them, almost daintily, to its maw. It worked so fast that the meat would be gone in seconds.

Then the banging will start again, and Sarah will start whining. Again.

New day, same old shit.

He hadn't told her about his idea.

It had come to him in a flash, just last night. Remarkably, he'd still been sober at around eight o' clock. He'd put on the television to avoid listening to Sarah's babbling about some new pair of shoes she was thinking of buying. The television was showing an old movie, about a travelling carnival.

"Come and see the only mermaid in captivity," a barker called, and the punters flocked to the booth. Dollar bills flowed like confetti at a wedding, even though the *mermaid* was obviously an old monkey with a cod's tail strapped to its ass. That didn't matter. "See the freaks" a large colourful sign had said. It was like a light-blub switching on above Joe Porter's head.

A crab that big has to be some kind of freak.

And straight after that thought there was another.

A lot of people would pay good money to see it. And maybe, just maybe, a zoo would pay good money to buy it.

The thought had kept him awake most of the night, lying there listening to the *thud* of pincer on glass and the *scurrying* of legs on rough sand. He'd got up and drank more whisky while watching the beast.

It kept banging on the glass.

Keep at it fucker. Grow big and strong. You're my meal ticket out of this shit-hole.

And even in the cold light of day, when sobriety started to creep close, the thought still wouldn't go away.

That fucker is getting huge. Some zoo will pay through the nose for it.

He'd noted down a list of possible numbers to call earlier. But he had no intention of telling Sarah. She'd want to share.

Fuck that for a game of soldiers. Once I get the cash I'm outa here like shit off a shovel. And I'm not taking anyone with me. Shit. The crab is probably more intelligent than she is.

He couldn't complain about the view though. Sarah was bent over the aquarium, tapping on the glass, amused, for a while, as the crab tapped angrily back. Denim cut-offs rode high on her buttocks and her tits hung heavy in a loose halter-top.

She saw him looking,

"Do you like?"

He grunted and took a swig of rum.

She stuck her tongue out at him and went back to teasing the crab.

Porter looked at the telephone. He couldn't wait any longer. The idea was too big in his head.

"Sarah?" he said.

She looked up expectantly, a smile starting.

"Fuck off for five minutes. I need to make a call."

He ignored the hurt look she threw at him as she went out onto the deck. He heard a splash as she dived into the water, and more splashes as her strong swimming stroke took her away from the shore. Once he was sure she was far out of hearing distance he picked up the phone.

Getting anyone to understand the power of his idea proved more difficult than he'd hoped. His first choice, the Queen's Zoo he remembered visiting as a child, turned him down flat after hardly twenty seconds. Central Park Zoo proved slightly better.

"It's a big crab you say?"

The voice on the other end of the line was a Doctor Newman, the third person he'd spoken to, and the only one so far to show even the *slightest* interest.

"It's a very big crab," Porter said. "You ain't never seen nothing like it."

"I doubt that very much," Newman said. His voice had a clipped nasal quality to it that immediately got on Porter's nerves. "But I'm certainly interested. Bring it to me in the morning and I'll give you a professional opinion."

"Can't you send someone out here?" Porter asked. "I told you… it's a big fucker."

Newman laughed but even on the end of a telephone line Porter could tell there was little that this man would *ever* find funny.

"No," he said bluntly. "It's your crab. Either bring it here, or keep it there. I don't really care either way."

If Porter had met Newman in a bar they would now be less than five seconds from a fight.

But I need that money.

He bit his lip and kept his temper.

"And if I bring it, you'll pay?" he asked, trying not to sound *needy.*

Newman sighed so loudly that Joe heard it on the line.

"Just bring it here. We can discuss a monetary arrangement if it does indeed prove to be as *special* as you say."

"I told you…"

Newman didn't give him a chance to finish.

"Yes, it's a *big fucker*. I heard you the first time. Just bring it."

Newman hung up.

Porter looked up from the phone to see the crab looking straight at him. It had developed a large pair of round staring eyes. It watched him, unblinking.

"Do you like?" Porter said in a high-pitched imitation of Sarah.

The crab banged hard on the glass. There was a loud crack and a spider web of fine lines appeared.

Little fucker will be far too strong soon.

But then the zoo could deal with it.

And I'll have the loot.

He took a long swig from the rum bottle.

"Okay doll," he shouted. "The coast is clear."

He heard more splashing outside. He headed for the door.

"Come on in Sarah," he shouted.

There was a louder splash, and a *clack* as loud as a gunshot.

Behind him, in the tank, the crab went wild, rapping ever harder against the glass. The cracks spread, but the glass held.

For now.

Sarah screamed, a high wail that chilled Porter all the way through despite the heat. He ran out onto the deck, and got there just in time to see a huge white claw grab the girl around the waist.

She looked straight at him and screamed.

"Do something!"

Porter couldn't get his legs to move. He stood, gaping in awe. The claw was near as long as Sarah herself. It had raised a wound around her waist that was already bleeding heavily. He could see a portion of the back of the crab. From what he could gauge it was more than six feet across.

"Help me Joe," Sarah screamed. "Help me."

A second claw raised high over her head and came down fast.

Snick.

Her head came cleanly off. Red froth bubbled as the torso aspirated water. The crab lifted the body above its head while the other claw *clacked* eagerly.

Snickety-snick.

Sarah's arm and half her rib cage fell into the bay. Most of her internal organs slithered behind with a soft splash that Porter was afraid he would be hearing in his dreams for the rest of his life.

A second snick and her legs fell, two separate splashes. The crab dropped the lump of meat that was all that remained of the stripper. It looked up. White eyes the size of saucers stared straight at Porter.

His legs still refused to move, even as the crab started to come towards the dock.

Time to get the fuck out of Dodge, Joe. Git moving.

Finally his legs agreed. He was headed for the back yard and the safety of his truck when he remembered the crab.

The thought of the zoo's money overrode his fear. He went back inside and lifted the aquarium tank off its legs. It was too heavy to carry, and he had to drag and manhandle it across the floor to the rear door. He eyed the crack warily, but it held.

For now.

The young crab beat a tattoo against the glass.

Clank, clank, clankety-clank.

Loud *clacking* from the Bay responded in time as Joe half-fell out into his back yard, dragging the tank behind him.

The clacking from the Bay on the other side of the cabin sounded like someone letting off a shotgun. He lifted the aquarium and heaved it into the back of his pickup, his heart leaping to his mouth as the tank tipped and almost spilled back to the ground. All the while the crab kept up the beat against the wall of the tank.

Outside on the front deck the newcomer pulled itself out of the water. Timber split and cracked as it attacked the front door area. The whole cabin swayed and groaned as the noise rose to a cacophony. Porter jumped into the pickup and slammed the door behind him. The rear view mirror showed timber and roof joists being flung aside like matchsticks. A huge claw waved in the air above the shack then came down with a *crash*. The shack sagged in the middle like a broken-backed horse. But it held… for now.

Porter had a bad moment when he thought the truck keys were still on the table in the kitchen. He had started to turn towards the door when he found them in his pocket. His hands shook, and he had to concentrate like a drunk finding a lock before he managed to turn them in the ignition.

More wood broke in the shack, loud *cracks* like gunfire.

The engine chugged but didn't take.

He tried again.

Still nothing.

"Come on you fucking piece of shit," he shouted

Behind him the huge crab smashed the back wall of the cabin onto kindling. The young crab rattled against the aquarium glass again, just as the pickup engine caught and Porter slammed his foot on the accelerator.

The big crab snapped its claws together, matching the rhythm coming from the tank.

Porter could still hear it as he drove away, even above the rattle of the old engine.

Click, click, clickety-click.

5

Shona spent a large part of the next two weeks studying the stomach contents of the whale. They only confirmed what she, and her father, already feared.

The stomach had been filled with partially digested fish, sea-urchins, large squid, a barrow-full of rock… and remnants of chitinous claws and shells. Shona hadn't needed to look at the pieces long to know what she looked at.

The crabs are back.

Their pieces were scattered, not just in the whale's stomach, but in the body cavity itself, and also in the lungs. The whale also seemed to be short of most of its blubber, only empty space where the fat layers should be. And there were bits of crab everywhere.

Judging by the size of some of the fragments she found, they were big.

Big as horses.

She showed Stark a white claw nearly four feet long.

"These things can produce thousands of pounds of pressure per square inch," she said. "Something this big would be capable of taking a modern car apart in seconds."

Stark whistled.

"Imagine what it would do to a body," he said.

Shona felt the chill in her spine again.

"I don't have to imagine. We've both seen the video evidence. I don't think there's any doubt what did the killings."

Stark fell quiet.

"It's what we feared. What are we looking at here? Are there more of them?"

Shona shrugged.

"At the moment there's no way of telling. But things that large will have left traces," she told Stack. "More traces than we have seen so far."

That had been several days ago. Stack had a squad of researchers working on reports of missing people or strange accidents at sea.

Shona was soon proved right. A pattern was starting to form. From the start some two months ago off Cuba they had been moving steadily northward and eastwards, coming up the coast in a slow but steady manner. They made infrequent forays ashore, as if checking, *or searching*, then went back to traveling.

Sometimes livestock had got in the way. Sometimes people.

Two more dead whales were found just a few miles further south, both burst open in the same way.

It was Shona's father who had made the leap of intuition.

They're hitching a ride. Like getting on a bus.

It was hard to imagine, and for Shona with her academic background, almost impossible to believe. It was attributing too much intelligence to something that just didn't have the nervous system to produce rational thought. She was trying to rationalise the behaviour as a newly learned instinct but that was just too much of a stretch.

And that's before I even think about how they survive inside a whale for weeks at a time!

But there was the evidence to consider… the pieces of claw and carapace scattered though the whale's body cavity. The scientist in her couldn't deny that.

I just can't explain it. Not yet.

As she knew he would, her father had several theories, most of which she found outlandish in the extreme.

"They're checking out breeding grounds," he said. That might well be the case, but he also thought there might be *thousands* of them, an army of sorts.

She refused to consider that idea. It was just *too* outlandish, too far from her view of how the world worked.

It doesn't stop Dad theorising though.

She'd spent several hours on the web-cam now, talking to him at his desk over in Scotland. It was the most they'd talked in ten years or more. Shona tried to keep it professional, but it was difficult. They had always knocked heads, as far back as Shona could remember. He was a hard man to love.

And a hard man to hate.

"Don't underestimate them," he said. "Remember the damage they've done in the past."

As if you'd ever let me forget.

The crabs had started showing up as far back as the '70s. Back then there had only been a few encounters with people. When one had first been caught there was a minor uproar in the press, but the papers soon went back to reporting on the doings of celebrities, and people forgot about the giant crabs, mutants born out of man's own love for chemicals and pharmaceuticals, beasts grown huge on the effluent purged from factories and water supplies all over the world.

Her father had retired several years ago, but he had been a Professor of Marine Biology at St. Andrews University for many years, and he had worked with the British authorities in the study of the crabs. *Secretly.* He'd seen at first hand the carnage and mayhem an infestation could cause when they attacked a small fishing community on the west coast of Scotland. Twenty years had since passed. It was covered up as best could be done, and most of the general public never even knew there was a possible problem.

And who was going to listen to the rantings of somewhat maverick scientist predicting a return of rampaging crustaceans? But the experience had changed him, turned him into the sort of wild-eyed opinionated madman you'd change seats to avoid on the subway. His retirement hadn't been voluntary, and he'd taken it hard. In recent years he'd become taciturn and withdrawn, but this latest possibility of an outbreak had him re-energised. The old fervour was back, and if Shona wasn't careful she'd be burnt by the intensity of it.

Since her first call, two weeks ago, Dad had got increasingly more animated, and it was all she could do to stop him jumping on a plane.

"You're retired Dad," she said. "Leave this to younger heads."

"You never retire from something like this," he said. And for the first time in her life she realised he was getting old. More than that, he was starting to look his age, and tired with it.

"You're better off over there," she said softly. "Besides. I'm with the Yanks. They've got enough weaponry to take anything down."

"Weaponry is no use without the skill to wield it." Dad said. "I've seen that myself."

Shona didn't doubt the skill of Stark's team. But they were getting twitchy at the lack of something to shoot at. They hadn't yet managed to find a single live specimen. She *had* found several piles of soft grey scat on the beach that told her that at least one of the attackers was bigger than any crab she had ever seen.

Much bigger.

They'd found several of the very large claws inside the dead whale, each nearly four feet long and eighteen inches wide. Shona had run extensive tests on them. They didn't tell her much that she didn't know already.

It's a crab claw. A bloody huge crab claw.

There was one other thing, something she had not even told her father yet. She'd only found it this morning and still didn't quite believe it. She sent the lab test back and had it done again. And again it came back with the same result.

Somehow evolution had given these crabs a new advantage in their anatomy.

Their shells are reinforced.

Shona tested the strength of a piece.

She hit it with a hammer. The tool bounced off, jerked out of her hand and almost took out a ten-thousand dollar microscope. It *did* smash into a row of test tubes, scattering glass everywhere.

Sergeant Matthews ran inside at the crash.

"Just the man," Shona said. She showed him the piece of shell. "I'm destruction testing this."

Matthews looked at the broken glass.

"Destruction seems the appropriate word. Let's see how it handles a real test."

He took out his pistol and fired at the shell from close range. The bullet left only a small gouge in the surface as it bounced off and tore a small hole in the roof of the tent.

Matthews bent over the shell.

"It's part of one of the crabs?"

Shona nodded.

He banged on the shell with the butt of the pistol. He didn't even make a dent.

"We're going to need bigger guns," the Sergeant muttered.

"My thoughts exactly," Shona said. "These things are going to be tougher to put down than I imagined."

Matthews turned the piece of shell over in his hand.

"If you *really* are destruction testing it, I've got a grenade somewhere?"

Shona nearly laughed.

"I think it has proved its point Sergeant, but thanks for the offer."

The Sergeant showed no sign of leaving.

"These crabs," he said. "How big do they get?"

She remembered some of Dad's stories.

"As big as a horse. Some even bigger."

The man went white.

"I've never liked crabs. All that sideways scuttling ain't natural. They give me the creeps. They're just too *different*."

Shona laughed.

"I'm the opposite. And for the same reason. I find them fascinating because of their differences."

Matthews wasn't convinced.

He holstered his pistol.

"Fascinating ain't a word I'd use for them. *Scary* is more like it."

Shona took the shell from him as he left. She was wondering just how big an advantage such armoury would give the beasts in the wild

Scary indeed. I'm starting to come round to the Sergeant's way of thinking.

She spent the next few hours trying to decipher the shell's secrets. She finally managed to scrape a piece off with the hammer and a chisel. Under high magnification it looked almost crystalline, a tightly woven network of chitin that reminded her of the extra-strong fibreglass used in ocean going hulls.

She kept going back and looking at it, just to make sure her eyes hadn't deceived her. She had trouble believing it. It represented a mutation that had leapt up from nowhere in a creature that was *already* a mutation.

And if that can happen, then anything can happen. All bets are off.

She'd just sat up from the microscope when Stark walked in. She smiled and he smiled back at her.

He should do that more often. It suits him.

"Any news?" she asked.

He shook his head.

"Maybe we've got lucky. Maybe they've gone back to wherever they came from?" he said.

Shona shook her head.

"With these beasts, we can't make any assumptions. Dad thinks they're on a hunt."

"For what?"

She shrugged.

"He says *breeding ground*. But I doubt we'll ever know. Unless they find it."

Stark sat beside her. She'd noticed over the past few days that he was *popping* in a lot, and staying longer each time.

"We've got the FEMA people on high alert all up the seaboard," he said. "Wherever they come ashore, we'll be ready."

Shona stayed quiet, remembering stories from her youth, of carnage and mayhem in seaside towns around the British coasts. It would do no good to tell Stark of her fears. He had the confidence that came with years of serving in the strongest military power on the planet. Thoughts of defeat would never even enter his head.

"So what next?" he asked her. "What else can we do?"

"Wait," she said. "And hope that, when it comes, we really *are* ready for it."

6

"What so you think of that sucker?" Porter said.

"Well, it certainly *looks* big enough," Newman replied.

The crab sat in the tank in the back of Porter's truck and stared balefully at them. It looked even angrier than ever. It waved a claw as if it was berating Porter for having brought it to this place.

He was glad to have finally got to the zoo. Even though he'd thrown a tarpaulin over the tank his old battered truck had drawn curious glances all the way through the city. Once, when he was stuck at a set of lights, the beast decided it was time to start banging again. The loud clanging drew the attention of a policeman but luckily for Porter the lights changed and he was able to pull away.

Now he was parked up in the zoo. He'd had a near fight with security before he finally convinced them he was *kosher.* And now he was finding out what he'd suspected on the phone. Newman was like oil to his water. He had the stuffy, tight air of a man with a corncob up his ass, and he spoke like a prissy schoolteacher. Porter felt like Newman expected him to scrape and bow.

Ain't never been one for much of that.

Newman had come running quick enough when told of the crab though.

I guess I caught his interest.

Porter could almost feel the money in his pocket already.

I got him on the hook. Time to reel him in.

"What have you been feeding it?" Newman said after studying the crab from all angles.

"Other crabs mostly. That, wieners and baloney."

"You give it junk food?"

Porter laughed.

"Why should it eat any better than the rest of us? It's none the worse for it. It's three times the size it was just two weeks ago."

"And you've never seen another like it?"

Years of playing poker with the Watts brothers allowed Porter to lie with a straight face.

"There ain't no other like it *Doctor*. What you have here is a one off. A freak of nature."

Newman leaned closed to the tank. The crab rapped hard on the glass and Newman stepped back, fast, almost tripping over his feet in his haste to retreat.

Rattled you, didn't he?

Newman made a play of cleaning his spectacles with a handkerchief to hide his discomfort.

Porter pressed his advantage.

"So what do you think? He must be worth *something* to you."

At the mention of money Newman quickly regained his composure.

"It's hardly unique," the man said. "I remember the stories from England, even if you don't. And supposedly they were *much* bigger than this one."

"Ah. But them's foreign parts," Porter said. "And this is Manhattan. Ain't never been one here."

Newman nodded. He seemed almost hypnotised by the crab. Likewise it sat and stared straight back at him.

"Maybe this *is* all you say it is. Time will tell. We'll keep it here under observation until we are sure of what we have."

Porter lowered his voice.

"What about our monetary arrangement?"

Newman still couldn't take his eyes off the crab.

"We shall see," Newman said. "Come back next week. If it has grown as you say it will, then we can make an agreement then."

Porter knew better than to push. That was something else he'd learned from the Watts brothers.

Softly, softly, catchee monkey.

7

Another ten days passed before the research team got a break.

Shona had actually began to relax, thinking that maybe it had all been a storm in a teacup, an aberrant resurgence of just a very small number of the crabs that had since retreated to some deep cold place in the ocean.

Dad, of course, was having none of it.

"Stay vigilant," he insisted, hectoring even over the internet link. "Don't let them give up searching. Not yet. It's too soon."

She had been surprised to find Stark in agreement.

"Losing the Seals has the brass spooked," he explained." We're not going anywhere until they get some answers."

So she kept sifting the clues, looking for something that would tell her where to look. She'd come up with nothing, and the frustration grew by the day. She was near bursting point on the tenth day when Stark strode into the tent.

Shona looked up from a specimen tray.

Stark looked happier than he had for days.

He's like a kid with a new toy. The promise of action has woken him up.

"Get your gear. We've got a lead," he said. "We have a report of a large pod of whales in distress off Long Island."

"*How* large?"

"Large," he said, and smiled. "Now are you coming, or should I just go on my own?"

"Just try to stop me," she said.

She grabbed her kit and followed Stark outside, just as the rotor of the waiting chopper started up. She almost laughed when she saw it. It was long, low and jet-black with no noticeable insignia.

He looked at her, an eyebrow raised.

"Is there a problem?"

She pointed at the chopper.

"Aren't black helicopters a bit of a cliché in your business?"

Stark *did* laugh.

"We've got an image to maintain. It adds to our mystique," he said. "Besides, we like cool toys. Mind your head."

They ducked below the rotors and headed for the chopper. Lieutenant Wilkes helped her on board. He shouted something at her but she couldn't make it out… the noise inside was almost deafening. Even when Stark handed her ear-mufflers and a communication headset it still sounded like she was inside a washing machine on a heavy load.

"You'll get used to it," Stark said over the headset. He sat opposite and tapped at his ear-muffler. "And at least with these you won't go deaf."

When the chopper started to rise she felt like she'd left her stomach behind. The vehicle lurched and suddenly Shona was afraid that she was going to throw up her breakfast. She sat quietly, as still as she could, until the feeling passed.

In the meantime she watched as Stark applied camouflage paint to his cheeks then stripped and reassembled a sub-machine pistol. On either side of him Matthews and Wilkes did the same. Wilkes slammed a magazine into place.

Stark saw her looking.

"The Sergeant told me about your experiment with the pieces of shell," he said. "I ordered armour-piercing rounds. I thought we might need them."

I hope you don't.

"What can we expect?" Wilkes asked. "I mean, if this is what you think it is?"

Shona didn't reply.

"Just be ready for anything," Stark said. "We're in an unknown situation, against an enemy we've never fought before. We need to stay sharp on this one."

The journey took over an hour, during which Shona had plenty of time to worry about what might wait at the other end. Her dreams had been troubled for days… full of *clacking* carnage, mayhem and the smell of blood. And she always came back to the two young girls in the water.

She had woken up screaming three nights in a row. Before the past few weeks she'd never *really* understood her father's obsession. All she knew was that it had driven a wedge between him and her mother. It was only now, many years on that her parents would even *talk* to each other. Dad had always been rushing all over the world to *investigate* the latest scare, most of which turned out to be false alarms. And all Shona knew was that her father would rather be chasing crabs than being with his daughter.

She'd taken up her area of research in a vain attempt to try to understand him.

Well girl, I would say you've finally got there.

And now his warnings echoed in her ears.

Don't underestimate them. Never underestimate them.

She was so far gone in her reverie that she jumped in her seat when Stark touched her shoulder.

"We're there."

She realised that the chopper had started to hover. There was sudden tension in the air. Wilkes and Matthews both gripped their weapons. The light above them turned from green to red, casting dark shadows on their faces, making their eyes into dark black pools. Shona had a premonition of doom, so strong that she felt like screaming.

But a Scotswoman's fancies won't cut the mustard with these guys.

She saw Stark listen to a voice in his ear-piece and watched as he went to the chopper door. He beckoned Shona forward as he opened it. She made her way gingerly across the aisle and looked out, aware that Stark had grabbed her tightly around the waist to keep her from tumbling out. It suddenly became more difficult to concentrate. But when she leaned out further all extraneous thoughts dissipated fast.

The chopper hovered above a long sandy spit. Ten large Sperm whales wallowed in the shallow water less than thirty yards offshore and ten yards below them. That alone made Shona suspicious. Sperm whales are rarely seen in groups, and certainly never more than two or three at a time.

And never, ever in water this shallow. It looks like they're trying to beach!

That wasn't the worst of it though. The whales were bloated, the thick skin of their stomachs stretched tight and ready to burst. Huge tails struck weakly at the water and the whale blow, usually metres high, was the merest puff of fish-smelling vapour.

A family, two adults and two young children, stood on the sand bar, pointing excitedly at the spectacle, the father holding a video camera. Once more Shona had a flashback to the scene on the video.

The water turns red. The splashing gets frantic, spray rising high, obscuring the view of what is happening. One of the girls screams, but the noise is quickly silenced. The camera drops to the sand, showing only a man running to where a red slick lies on the water.

Even as she remembered, the man below her started walking closer to the whales.

No. Not again.

"We need to go down," Shona shouted. "Take us down. There are kids down there."

Stark talked to the pilot, but Shona couldn't take her eyes from the people below. The chopper whipped up waves as it descended and the family backed away from the machine.

No. Not that way! They're moving closer to the whales.

She called out.

"Get away. Get back!"

But her voice was whipped away, lost beneath the sound of the rotors.

"They won't hear you," Stark said in her ear. "Just hold on. We'll be there in seconds."

The belly of the nearest whale ripped. A large bloody claw, larger even than the one she had back at the lab, poked from the wound and started to snip.

We don't have seconds.

"Get us down!" she shouted at Stark. "Faster. Time's up."

Stark pulled her back from the doorway. She saw his eyes go wide with surprise. But it didn't slow him down. He had his gun up and aimed in less than a second.

He leaned out and started firing. The noise reverberated and rang through the chopper and even through the mufflers Shona feared she might have gone deaf.

"We have a go," he shouted. Wilkes and Matthews moved to stand behind him and Shona had to step aside to give them room. The chopper banked suddenly, forcing her to sit down heavily in a seat to avoid falling. Stark never even broke from firing.

He was still shooting as he jumped out of the door. The other two men left straight after him. Shona wondered whether she should join them, but before she could get off the chair and move back to the door the chopper rose again.

She heard gunfire from outside. Swaying alarmingly due to the motion, she pulled her way back to the doorway.

I should have asked for a gun.

Stark and the other officers stood between the whales and the family, ankle deep in the water at the shore. Thirty yards away the whales bulged and contorted. Gore flew in the air as crabs, tens of them, slashed and hacked their way out of the stomach and chest cavities. Some of the crabs were as big as cows. They were red legged, with deep-purple shells and long pincers, cream-coloured, like aged ivory. Claws rose in the air and *clacked.*

They tore savagely at the whale meat and pulled themselves, dripping, out of the gore. They seemed to be acting in concert, forming a defensive line in front of the whales while more cut their way out behind them. Bullets flew, but it didn't seem to slow them.

A large group of the beasts headed away, moving further along the coast. That still left Stark and his men facing a score or more.

The crabs raised their claws in the air as if in salute, then, as one, attacked. The three men pumped round after round into the beasts. Bullets bounced off shells and claws. Some punctured the soft tissue at eyes and joints in legs and mandibles, but the wave of crabs barely slowed, bearing down fast on the three men.

They're using armour-piercing rounds. And they hardly leave a scratch!

Stark shouted an order that she couldn't hear above the din.

Wilkes and Matthews turned and ran, grabbing the children and hustling the parents, trying to get them out of the crab's path. Stark stood his ground.

The crabs were barely ten yards from him, and still he stood alone, strafing the advancing beasts with long bursts.

Shona saw him take something from his belt and throw it in the water, then he too turned and ran.

Seconds later there was a blinding *flash* and a *whump* as a grenade went off. The chopper was buffeted from side to side in the shock wave, throwing Shona heavily to the floor. When she recovered and dragged her way back to the door she saw pieces of claw and shell scattered over a wide area of the sea and shore.

But Stark had only slowed the beasts, not stopped them. A dozen or more of the crabs still waded in the shallows, intent on getting to the small group of fleeing people.

"Get us down," she screamed. "We need to rescue them. Now!"

She wasn't sure if she'd been heard, but the pilot obviously got the idea as he banked the chopper over the top of the crabs and positioned himself further away down the shore. They hovered, eight feet off the ground. Beneath them sand was whipped up into spinning vortices.

Shona leaned as far out of the door as she dared.

"Run!" she shouted.

Stark was the closest to the chopper. He tried to aim and fire his pistol while running full pelt through soft sand. Behind him Wilkes carried a child while Matthews, already carrying the other child, attempted to help the mother, half-carrying her in a limping run. The father lagged behind, struggling to make his way through the sand, already red faced and breathing hard. The crabs scuttled, mere yards behind him, pincers already reaching for his legs, clacking in frustration, just inches away from snagging him.

Hurry! For God's sake, hurry!

Stark reached the chopper first. He took the kid from Wilkes and tossed it up to Shona. She placed him in a seat. The boy was shaking with fear, and tears ran down dust-smeared cheeks. Shona went back to the door and reached out a hand to Stark, but he had already turned back.

Wilkes had doubled back to take the second kid from Stark. He was already near the chopper but Matthews and the others were still twenty yards away. Stark set up a covering fire, strafing the crabs behind the father, but the machine pistol didn't have enough stopping power. Shona realised there was no space to use another grenade -- not without killing the lagging man.

Wilkes reached the door and boosted the second kid up. The boy clambered aboard. Shona helped him into a seat next to his brother. When she turned back Stark was already in the chopper, hauling their mother aboard. Wilkes jumped up beside her. Stark and Wilkes leaned out of the door, firing smoking pistols down into the throng of crabs.

The noise of *clacking* claws was audible even above the roar of the chopper.

The father was next. He tried to leap up to the doorway. Stark caught his hand and the man yelled as he swung wildly to one side.

"Boost him up Sergeant. Quickly." Stark yelled. Shona couldn't see down beyond the sill of the door, but she guessed that the last soldier was down there beneath the man. The father's round red face showed in the doorway. He heaved and pulled but he just didn't have the strength to pull himself up. Stark had to lay down his pistol and grab the man with both hands.

Suddenly a burst of gunfire came from below. It was quickly followed by a piercing scream.

Stark's eyes took on a terrible, dead, look. Shona realised what that meant.

We just lost Matthews.

Stark grabbed at the father's arm higher up towards the shoulder and started heaving.

"Hey. Be careful," the big man shouted, pain showing on his face. "That's…"

Snick.

It sounded like a pair of scissors being closed.

The big man's face contorted in a mixture of new pain and shocked surprise. He jerked his head from side to side, then again more frantically. Blood burst from his mouth. His lips moved, but no sound came out.

Stark gave his arm one more heave. It was easier than before. Head and shoulders flopped into the chopper… but that was just about all that was left of him. Below chest level the body was gone. Viscera hung in ropy strands, a coil of intestine lying like a wet sausage on the floor.

One of the kids screamed.

Stark wiped the back of his hand across his lips. He looked at Shona, then at the kids. He let go of what was left of their father and kicked out at the lolling head. The remains tumbled away out of sight leaving a bloody smear in the doorway.

"Take us up," Stark shouted in his mouthpiece. "Get us out of here."

The chopper started to rise. There was a screech of metal as something *scraped* across the bottom, then they were up and away. Wilkes gave the *OK* symbol with his thumb and first finger.

We made it.

Shona checked on the mother. She was uninjured, but her eyes had gone wide, pupils zoomed down into pinpoints.

She's in shock. And so are the kids.

Stark leant out the door as the chopper ascended. He kept firing until his pistol ran empty. Even then he kept pulling the trigger of the smoking gun until Shona put a hand on his arm.

"We're free. We made it," she said, aloud this time.

He looked at her, not seeing.

The family are not the only ones in shock.

Finally his eyes cleared.

"Matthews didn't make it. He's only been married a year," he said. "His wife is pregnant. How do I tell her? *What* do I tell her?"

Shona had no answer for him. She went back to check on the kids, swapping places with Wilkes as he went to stand at the door beside Stark. The Lieutenant looked out.

"The other crabs are on shore," he said. "They're swarming around the remains of a cabin."

Shona knew she should join him and check on the beasts' behaviour. But she couldn't take her gaze away from the wide-eyed stares on the faces of the children.

Now I know really how Dad feels.

8

Porter sat in the bar and fumed.

Fucking Zoo.

He downed a shot of straight rum and banged the glass on the counter repeatedly until the barman brought him another. The barman looked like he was just about pissed off enough to say something, but one look from Porter put paid to that.

Don't fuck with me. Not if you want to have any teeth left.

The two seats on either side of him were empty, and had been since he *snarled* at a suit who had tried to make conversation. Some days bars were for jawing, other days, for drinking.

Today is most definitely a drinking day. And it's all that bastard Newman's fault.

It was nearly ten days now since Porter delivered the crab, and still Newman refused to pay out.

"We can't be sure it's not just a big crab," he said, that very morning, when Porter went to the aquarium for the third time in as many days.

"Can't be sure?" Porter said, pointing at where the crab bashed against the glass of its aquarium. "Look at the fucker. It's more than three feet across!"

"Big, yes," Newman said in that prissy voice that was starting to get on Porter's nerves. "But still not outside the parameters of normality for a crab of this type."

"*Of this type?* What type is that then?" Porter said. "Go on, you're the fucking *Doctor*. Educate me."

Newman sighed, and once more he looked like a schoolteacher, disappointed in an unruly pupil. Porter had seen more than enough of that look in his own schooling, thank you very much.

"You must understand…" Newman started.

"Oh, I *understand.* I understand you're trying to screw me over."

Newman put a hand on his arm and led him away from the tank. Porter noticed that the crab watched him intently, following his every move.

The little snapping fucker knows me.

"It will just be a few days longer Mr Porter," the man said. "Then you'll have your money, and I will have my exhibit."

Porter shrugged Newman's arm off his shoulder.

"You have three days more *Doctor* Newman, he said. "And if you don't have twenty thousand dollars for me, I'll be taking *my* exhibit elsewhere."

Newman merely smiled, a thin, humourless thing that Porter felt like spreading across his face. He could feel the anger rising up inside him.

Softly, softly.

He didn't *feel* like going softly, but he forced the rage down, for a while at least, and turned away.

As he left the crab raised a claw and bashed, hard, on the glass, as if summoning him to return. Porter looked back. It hit the glass again.

A large crack ran from floor to ceiling.

"I think we may need a larger tank," Newman said, smiling.

The bastard is jerking my chain.

Porter struggled to contain himself. He had learned from past fuck-ups that punching out the money *before* you got paid was never a good idea.

He had taken his rage and headed for the nearest bar.

He'd almost turned and walked out again when he saw the pole dancer on a tiny stage down the far end. She looked too much like Sarah, and that was a thought he'd been trying hard to dismiss. He was okay in daylight hours, but nights were taking way too much rum to get through. Every time he closed his eyes he saw it.

"Help me Joe," she screamed. "Help me."

And then the sound, the one he'd been hearing, the one that even a pint of rum wouldn't drown.

Snick.

He tried to tell himself he didn't care.

Hell, I've been trying that all my goddamn life.

But Sarah's face kept coming back to mind. He missed her. It had taken a while for him to accept it, but there it was. He watched the dancer for long seconds.

Sarah was better.

He'd met her in a bar much like this, on another day that was *made* for drinking. At that time he'd been holding down a construction job over in Queens, but the foreman had a smart mouth and Porter had never been one to listen to smart mouths for too long.

One punch later and he was out of a job and into the nearest bar.

And there she was. More legs than she would ever need, and breasts that just begged to be fondled. He'd got drunk and given her just enough money to get her interested.

Then he'd spent a year treating her like shit. But still she stayed.

Then I had to go and catch that little fucker.

He'd been wondering a lot about that. It was surely too much of a coincidence that the bigger crab had turned up when he had the smaller one.

It was searching for it. And found Sarah.

He closed his eyes to hide sudden tears, but the images were there, waiting, just behind his eyelids.

A claw raises high over her head and comes down fast.

Snick.

Her head comes cleanly off. Red froth bubbles as the torso aspirates water. The crab lifts the body above its head while the other claw clacks eagerly.

Snickety-snick.

His eyes snapped open. He remembered, all too well, what came next. He doubted he'd ever forget it.

I miss her.

The thought hit him, hard. And suddenly Porter was angry again… with himself this time.

The dancer smiled at him.

She looks nothing like Sarah. When Sarah smiled, she meant it.

He had walked to the bar and sat with his back to the dancer.

The self-pity and rage drained out of him as the rum did its job, but the hate for Newman came back, and the thought of the money was almost too big to contain in his head. Since then five straight rums hadn't improved his mood any, and he needed to slow down, otherwise he'd be too drunk to move in an hour.

That might not be a bad idea.

He hadn't been back to the cabin. He'd been living out of a room round the corner from where he sat, a fleapit that had a bed, a head and a television that was either too quiet or too loud and gave everyone a bright-red face. Going back there didn't appeal.

Not when there was plenty of liquor to be had here.

He raised the rum to his lips, then thought better of it and turned his attention to the large television above the bar.

"In Breaking News tonight. Twelve mature sperm whales have washed ashore in Bellport Bay. Authorities are on the scene but details are sketchy as to the cause of this beaching. An Exclusion Zone has been thrown up around the area and sightseers have been asked to stay away until any possible threat to public safety has been identified. We understand that marine biologists are currently studying the animals to determine cause of death."

The picture was blurred and out of focus, taken from high above. It showed little more than a dozen long black blobs lying just off a beach. What caught Porter's attention was the chopper on the beach. Long, low and black, it didn't look like anything a marine biologist would use.

That's military, or I'm a fucking Dutchman.

The report continued.

"In a related story, another cabin has been found demolished on the Bellport shore, bringing the total to three in the past two weeks. Police continue to be baffled as to the cause. They are treating it, and the others, as an extreme act of vandalism, and possibly a series of revenge attacks by a gang with a grudge. But a police spokesman today admitted that they have no idea what, or who, might be behind it."

I do.

Something was going down out in the Bay, and Porter had a good idea what the cause might be. He drained his glass.

"More rum," he called, and banged the glass on the bar. This time the barman did not dare to even look at him the wrong way.

I need to get that cash. If I don't get it soon Newman will be able to just walk down to Bellport Bay and pick up one of the fuckers for himself.

9

They set up a field unit on the shore of Bellport Bay near the carcasses of the whales. Stark asked Shona to stay inside while they cleaned up the beach.

"Sergeant Matthews deserves some respect," he had said. "I mean to make sure he gets it."

Shona busied herself getting trestles up, then setting up the equipment that was coming in from the previous site. The routine of it started to calm her, taking the edge off the horror she'd witnessed in the chopper.

But I'll never forget the eyes of the children.

Outside she could hear soldiers working but she didn't look out, afraid of what gruesome horror might lie there.

She'd looked out once, just in time to see them load some too-small bundles into a military ambulance. Then she was kept busy as they brought her what was left of the crabs that had died in the earlier melee. Soon she had several trestles full of shell, legs and claws and although the tent was well aired the smell started to tickle at her nostrils and at the back of her throat.

She was on edge, expecting at any moment to hear the dreaded *clackety-clack.* But there had been no more sign of the crabs all day. They had vanished as quickly as they had come. Stark had several units out on patrol boats, and seismic survey teams trawling the length of the Bay, but so far with no results.

Shona looked up from the samples as Stark entered the tent.

The man was frustrated, and it showed as he walked briskly towards her. He had death in his eyes, and was spoiling for a fight.

"Matthews was a good man. I mean to avenge him."

"They're just dumb beasts," Shona said. "There was no malice in what they did. It's just their nature."

He rounded on her, eyes full of rage, and pain.

"It doesn't make him any less dead. I mean to lay waste to these *beasts* of yours."

She backed away from him, and he must have noticed that he had frightened her, as his voice softened, but his eyes held no less intensity.

"We've got enough firepower now to take out a small country," he said. "Let's see how the fuckers like *that*."

She put a hand on his arm.

"I'm sorry about the Sergeant," she said softly.

Stark touched her hand, stroking it, as if it was a well-behaved pet.

"Me too," he said, then moved away, suddenly embarrassed.

"What have you got for me?" he said. The officer in him was back.

She tried to keep it light.

"Bits of crab," she said. "Fancy some supper?"

She got a glimpse of a smile, but no more than that. He sat beside her and ran a hand through his hair.

There was a long silence. She found that she wanted to touch him again, to comfort him. But he was so wound up that she feared he might just explode. She went back to her microscope and pretended to study what was on the slide. After a while he started to speak, keeping his voice low as if afraid to be overheard.

"Matthews has been with me for five years. *Had* been with me. He was on my squad for every firefight I've been in. We saved each other's lives several times over, and got drunk as skunks afterwards. I was there when he won a hundred grand in Vegas and lost it all in an hour. I stood at his side at his wedding, and I was to be godfather to the first child. He was my friend."

Shona didn't trust herself to look up from the microscope. It was a full minute before Stark continued, and when he did there was a sob in his voice.

"The only bit of him I recognised was his hand… and that was only because his watch was still on the wrist. The crabs did a real number on him. We found one of his legs two hundred yards away down the shore. And we still haven't found the head…. I'm not sure I want to."

He went quiet again. Shona wanted desperately to go to him, but sensed now was not the time. Stark needed to grieve.

"That night in Vegas was the best night of his life. You should have seen him Shona…"

Shona smiled. That was the first time he'd called her that… and he hadn't even noticed. He was far away, in a casino on the other side of the country.

She let him talk and busied herself with routine; washing, packing and logging the samples. The story he told was a good one, full of bawdy humour and good cheer. When it ended he had tears running down his cheeks.

She pretended not to notice.

After a while Stark looked up. His eyes were red-rimmed, but clear.

"Thanks," he said.

"I didn't do anything," she replied.

He smiled.

"Yes. You did."

He stood, straightened up, and the Colonel was back again.

"So have you finished pretending to look in the microscope yet?"

She laughed.

"Not quite. These samples are the only evidence we've got. I'm hoping they'll tell us something… like where they came from. Or where they're going."

"Where the hell *did* they go?" he said softly. "Things *that* big surely can't hide for long."

"It's a big sea," she replied. "And they're cunning bastards."

"Is that the technical term?" Stark said, and smiled. "But surely they've got hardly any brain to speak of? How cunning can they be?"

Once more she heard her father's words.

Don't underestimate them.

"Obviously more than smart enough to figure out how to hitch a ride on a whale, then keep themselves hidden from view at the end of the journey. Any joy at the demolished cabins?" she asked.

He shook his head.

"There's three missing. Two crab fishermen, and an *exotic dancer.* We found bits of her. And other bits that look like they've been eaten."

His voice was hushed.

"Are these things man-eaters?"

Shona nodded, remembering more of the tales her father told if you gave him enough to drink.

"They developed a taste for it years ago."

"And you still think they're on a hunt?"

"Yes. I'm getting more and more convinced. The way they systematically went over those cabins was a sure sign. They're after something."

He looked up sharply.

"Surely they're not smart enough to be searching the whole stretch of the North Eastern seaboard?"

I hadn't thought so. Until now.

"I think they're smarter than we give them credit for," she said.

"But not all as big as others," a voice said from the tent entrance.

Lieutenant Wilkes stood there, carrying a solid plastic box, holding it away from his body as if scared of the contents.

"We found these," he said. "In the stomach of one of the whales."

Shona took the container from him and went to open it.

"Careful," Wilkes said. He held up a hand to show three bandaged fingers, fresh blood already seeping through. "They're vicious little bastards."

Shona looked through the side panel.

Three young crabs immediately rushed towards her, banging against the side of the container with claws that already looked like fearsome weapons.

"*These* were inside the whales?"

"There were many more," Wilkes said. "Most got away in the water before we could catch them, and just as many again are lying dead and chopped to bits in the stomach lining."

Shona put the container down and watched the crabs closely.

As if they had got bored with her, the three crabs stopped, standing still, claws raised in the air.

Are they tasting something? Or listening for something?

As one, the crabs started to clack their claws together in rhythm.

Click, click, clickety-click.

Then, still as one, they started to assault the left-hand side of the container.

"I've seen this before," Shona said softly, almost to herself. "They're following orders. There's something in that direction they *need* to get to."

10

Porter spent the best part of the next three days drunk as a skunk. Most of the time he sat in the same place in the same bar. When that lost its charms he bought a quart of rye and retired to the squalor of his room, watching re-runs of cop shows on cable and eating junk food.

The thought of the money he might get from the zoo rarely left him. He spun fantasies in his mind as to how he'd spend it, how it was going to change his life.

He arrived at the aquarium on the morning of the fourth day with a stinking hangover and high hopes.

He was to be disappointed, again.

It started as soon as he arrived at the main gates. The jumped-up guard wouldn't let him in, even after Porter gave him Newman's name. He was made to kick his heels in the road for the length of two smokes while the smirking gorilla made a series of increasingly lengthy phone calls.

After he was grudgingly granted admission he still couldn't find Newman. At the front gate, they'd told him to meet Newman in the aquarium. But when he got there the man was nowhere to be found.

And there's no way I'm going back to the gate. That gorilla has had all the satisfaction out of me he's gonna get.

He went in search of the money, not the man. He started by heading for the crab tank where he'd previously met Newman. The crack in the glass had widened and smaller cracks ran all over the surface. But the tank was empty. Neither the man nor the beast was anywhere to be seen.

Porter hailed a janitor who was mopping up further along the hall.

"Where's the crab gone?" he said.

The janitor made a motion with his mop, pointing to a corridor beyond.

"They done moved it. Damned good thing too. That thing was giving me the *heebee-jeebees…* kept watching me, as if I was going to be dinner, and banging on the glass like a drunk chimpanzee. They put up a bigger tank through the back. They're taking it through now."

Porter went along the corridor fast and went through a door at the far end. He arrived on the floor of a large hall he'd never been in before, a huge arena of metal girders and concrete.

It had obviously been set up as an exhibition area for one prize exhibit. Pictures of huge crabs lined the walls, the photographs all taken to show them off at their most menacing and vicious. A lot of time and money had been spent setting up the area.

We can't be sure.

That's what Newman had said. And all the time he'd been preparing the exhibition space, getting ready to fleece the punters with a modern-day freak show,

He's been dicking me around the whole time. Fucker.

Suddenly Porter was angry, and spoiling for a fight.

Any fight.

"Don't drop it," someone shouted.

Porter looked to his right.

Newman stood off to one side. Four grey-clad workmen gingerly carried a large meshed-steel cage. The crab sat inside, silent, watching proceedings with an unblinking stare.

The door that Porter had just come through screeched as it swung shut.

The crab turned its stare in his direction. And immediately went berserk.

Snick, snick, snickety snick.

Pincers tore at the steel mesh of the cage. The metal bent. A strand pinged as it was severed. Then another.

The man at the far corner had seen enough. He dropped his end of the cage. The unbalanced weight was too much for the other three to handle. They staggered, almost comically, around the floor, trying to keep on an even keel.

"Be careful you idiots," Newman shouted

Snick, snick.

The steel strands parted. One of the pincers pushed its way out, tearing the mesh aside as if it were wet paper. The crab attacked the metalwork with ever increasing frenzy.

"Screw this," one of the remaining workmen shouted and dropped the cage. He was off and away down the corridor before it hit the floor.

The other workmen let go of their end and stepped back.

The crab pushed its way out of the cage, effortlessly bending the last pieces of metal aside. It stood up high on its legs, raising the pincers above its head and showing its belly.

Clickety-clack.

Porter tensed, expecting an attack.

None came.

The crab looked straight at him for several seconds before moving. It bent closer to the floor and scuttled to one side, legs *clicking* on the concrete like the rapid rattle of a pair of knitting needles. It came to a stop next to a metal girder.

"Catch it you idiots," Newman shouted.

One of the workmen walked towards the crab, hands outstretched, appealing to it as if it was a cornered dog.

"Come on," he said softly. "There's nothing to be afraid of."

Oh yes, there is.

Porter would have called out, but an eerie silence had fallen. Every man was transfixed by the sight. The crab once more stood high on its legs and raised the pincers.

The man moved closer and put out his hand.

"See?" he said. "Nothing to be scared of."

Snick.

His right arm was taken off just above the elbow. Blood gushed in a high spray, spattering across the glossy photographs.

Someone screamed.

The injured man backed away and slumped against a pillar, left hand grasping at the stump, trying vainly to stem the blood that was already pooling on the floor at his feet.

The crab lifted a claw and banged, hard, on the nearest metal girder, one of the uprights holding up the building.

Clack, clack, clackety-clack.

Clack, clack, clackety-clack.

The noise rang and echoed like gunshots in the enclosed area.

Porter backed away towards the door.

I want no part of this fucking nonsense.

The crab turned its gaze on him. It raised itself to its full height, both claws *clacking*.

It launched itself straight at him.

11

Shona watched the small crabs closely. They stopped attacking the container and stood still again, pincers raised. All three were slightly tilted towards the left-hand corner of their prison.

Again? Can they really be listening? Or am I anthropomorphising?

As if on cue they moved back to the container wall, slightly to one side from their previous position. They beat on the plastic, all in rhythm.

Clack, clack, clackety-clack.

Clack, clack, clackety-clack.

"What are they doing?" Stark asked.

I have no idea.

I'm supposed to be the expert, and I have no idea.

The crabs paused, then attacked the case with renewed vigour. Small pieces of plastic flew in a whirl. Shona studied it closely. It looked like the container would hold them.

For a while at least.

She looked along their line of attack, raised her arm, and pointed in the direction.

"What's over there?" she asked Stark.

He had gone pale.

"Manhattan," he whispered.

12

Porter backed away quickly out the door as the crab scuttled towards him. He made it just in time… it slammed into the other side almost immediately. He grabbed the handle and stood, holding the door closed as the crab assaulted the wood on the other side.

Splinters flew.

One of the heavy pincers hit the security glass, sending a network of cracks running through it, turning clear glass to opaque.

A man-shaped shadow loomed behind the crab.

With any luck it's Newman. The fucker deserves to lose an arm or a leg.

But he could see enough to tell that the man wore the grey overalls of one of the workmen.

Through the door he heard Newman shout.

"Get it. Catch it!"

Snick.

The noise was loud even through the thick door.

Blood *splashed* across the glass and someone screamed, high and long.

Snick.

The screaming stopped.

The crab attacked the door again.

That was enough for Porter. He let go of the door and ran. Before he was ten yards down the corridor the door slammed open with a crash. He had a quick look back. The crab scuttled out, pincers raised. Fresh blood dripped from the edges.

Click, click, clickity click.

Again it saw Porter and made straight for him.

Fucker's got a hard-on for me.

Porter turned and fled. He heard the snicker of its legs on the concrete as it came after him.

I need a weapon.

He ran.

The crab ran faster.

He began to feel the effects of too many days of hard drinking. His stomach roiled and tumbled. His breath came hot and heavy.

I'm not going to get far.

The corridor stretched away to a door at the far end, and he wasn't convinced he was going to make it.

Snick.

He felt it tug at his heel.

It spurred him on to a spurt of speed, just enough to keep him ahead for several seconds longer. He reached the doorway and barrelled through it. He wasted several seconds looking for something with which to block the door.

There was nothing available.

He stood in an aquarium hall, a long thin dark space flanked on either side by the aquamarine glow of large tanks. Several zoo visitors were up the far end of the hall, but there was no one in the immediate vicinity.

The crab came through the door fast, hitting it with enough force to knock it from its hinges. Further up the hall heads turned at the sound of the crash

Clack.

The crab snapped a huge pincer towards Porter. He felt the breeze in front of his face.

He backed away, keeping his eyes on the crab. He knew that it would only take one mistake on his part and he'd be dead.

The crab banged loudly on the floor with a huge heavy pincer.

Clank, clank, clankety-clank.

An answering set of dull thuds came from a tank to Porter's right. He risked a look.

A large octopus, red and warty, thrashed violently, battering repeatedly against the glass. The whole tank shook. The crab turned in that direction. As soon as it spotted the octopus it flew into a rage, pincers clicking furiously. It threw itself at the tank, and with one thwack smashed the glass to small pieces.

A flood of water gushed across the floor, soaking Porter's feet up to the ankles.

The octopus landed with a wet *flop*, and in one fluid movement wrapped itself around one of the pincers and made its way down towards the crab's head. Muscle *flexed.* The octopus seemed to be on a mission to tear the crab to pieces.

Porter backed away, but the crab wasn't finished with him yet. Even as the octopus got a tentacle between a leg and the carapace and tried to prise its shell apart, still the crab lunged towards him. The free pincer *clacked*, once more just inches from his nose.

The octopus was now draped all over the top of the shell. It *pulsed*, like one huge muscle, and tipped the crab onto its back. Legs and pincers waved in the air as the beast tried to right itself.

Get the fucker.

But Porter was premature in celebrating. The free pincer found, then tore at, the octopus flesh. Pieces of rubbery tissue flew.

The crab rolled and righted itself.

Snick. Snick.

It methodically tore the octopus into small pieces.

It looked around, found Porter, and came forward again.

Porter backed off slowly. He knew he had nowhere to go, and the run along the corridor had taken almost all the energy he had in him. He raised his arms, already knowing they'd be worse than useless to defend him against the pincers. One of the huge claws came for him.

Crack!

A blast rang in Porter's ear. Two security guards arrived at his side, pistols raised. A bullet bounced off the shell, then another.

The crab stood up to its full height.

A bullet struck it in the belly. It didn't leave a hole, but it did manage to knock the creature backward. It righted itself, scuttled sideways, and moved rapidly through the wreckage of the broken octopus tank.

It was soon lost from sight in the darkness beyond.

Porter turned away and threw up all over the remains of the octopus.

When he stood he almost hit Newman who had run in from the opposite direction.

"What did you do?" the man shouted. Porter thought he looked a prime candidate for a heart attack, red faced and breathing heavily. "Look at this mess. It will take weeks to clean it up."

It was only then that he saw the dead octopus.

He turned on Porter again.

"You can forget getting any money out of me now. Get out of here, before I call the cops on you."

"We had a promise," Porter said softly. "I delivered my end of the bargain."

Newman waved his arms.

"You delivered a mess that'll cost me a small fortune. Where shall I send the bill? And where is the crab?"

One of the security guards pointed at the ruin of the empty tank.

"It went through that way Doctor."

Newman turned on Porter.

"You're the crab catcher aren't you? Get that fucking thing back here."

13

Shona watched the crabs as they tried to fight their way out of the container. She'd studied crabs all over the world.

But I've never seen such ferocity.

Her father had tried to warn her, but she hadn't listened. She'd always imagined that his stories were just that… stories, tall tales embellished by whisky to keep a young girl scared and entertained.

Scared, certainly. But entertainment seems some way off.

Stark still stood at her shoulder.

"If those things we saw out on the shore reach Manhattan…"

His voice tailed off. But he didn't need to complete the sentence. Shona could already see the scenes in her mind… there would be panic and slaughter on the streets of New York.

"There's a fleet of choppers available to us," Stark said. "But we need to know where to look."

Shona still couldn't take her eyes from the small crabs.

"Choppers won't do any good. These beasts like it dark. Dark and cold. Sewers and tunnels are where we should be looking."

Stark laughed bitterly.

"Well that narrows it down," he said sarcastically. "Manhattan doesn't have many of *those*."

Stark was a bundle of nervous energy. Shona had seen his type before, men of action, slightly lost when they had nothing to strike out at. But now she was starting to worry that the action he sought was not too far off.

She hadn't realised just *how* close.

Wilkes came in at a hurry, his face slightly flushed.

"We've got a bunch of hits on the tag cloud," he said. "Cell phone and internet traffic just spiked. There's a crab loose in Central Park."

14

Porter's first instinct was to get into his truck and get the fuck out of Dodge. Then the thought of the cash took hold again.

And Newman is right. I'm a crab-catcher. Best damned one on the shore.

He looked Newman in the eye.

"You'll pay me if I get it back. Fifty thou' sounds about right." Porter said.

It wasn't a question.

"It was twenty. That was to be our agreement."

"*Agreement?* Did our *agreement* cover you screwing me over? Did our *agreement* specify I should bend over and let you butt-fuck me? No. I think our *agreement* has gone the way of that there octopus. It's fifty thou' or I walk."

Newman looked white around the gills and had barely taken his eyes off the remains of the octopus.

"Just catch it," he whispered. "Before it kills anything else."

"A deposit would come in handy? As security?"

Newman gave him a thin smile. He had his composure back.

"Don't push your luck. Fifty it is. But I need it alive. And unharmed."

Porter turned to the security guards.

"Where does that go?" he asked, pointing at the space behind the ruined octopus tank.

The younger of them replied. He looked to be barely out of high school. His face had gone pale, which only served to show up his livid acne.

"It goes down into the workings. There's miles of piping and cabling down there. All the way down to the subway. You ain't getting me to chase that *thing* through that lot."

I ain't asking you to, son.

"I need some bait," Porter said. "Fish is good. Eel is better."

Newman looked grim.

"I'll see what I can do."

Porter looked past Newman to the far end of the hall. A crowd of the public had gathered. Cameras flashed, and two other security guards were hard pressed to hold the crowd back.

"And get the punters out of here," Porter said. "Maybe close the zoo down for the day?"

Newman looked like Porter had just said something disgusting.

"It's one of the busiest days of the summer."

Porter laughed.

"My point exactly. If a dead octopus makes you shake at the cost, just think the stink a dead child would cause."

Porter hadn't thought it possible, but Newman went even more pale. He left at a run, barking orders.

Porter put him out of mind.

Time to shit or get off the pot.

"I'll need a new cage," Porter said to the young security guard. "And I'll need it brought in here."

"What about out in the open?"

Porter shook his head.

"The little fuckers like it dark. They're sneaky."

But I'm sneakier.

He strode over to the octopus tank and looked through the back. The guard had been right. Behind the tank was a mess of wires and piping. He heard a noise in the far distance; the now instantly recognisable *clacking* of pincers.

"I'll also need a length of chain or thick rope," he said. "And a winch."

"You going to kill it?" the guard said.

Not if I can help it. Fifty thou' is going to buy me a whole heap of sunshine.

The bait arrived in two buckets a couple of minutes later. Somebody had chopped up a large eel.

Conger, by the looks of it. That should do the trick.

When the trap and gear turned up Porter set about attaching the bait to the end of the chain links. He carried it with him and walked through the broken tank. Glass tinkled underfoot and water seeped into his shoes and socks.

He stood at the far lip of the tank and looked into the darkness beyond. He remembered his own words.

The little fuckers like it dark. They're sneaky. But I'm sneakier.

He walked as far as he could see into the darkness. He put the chain down, checking there would be no snags when he had to haul it in. Crabs were generally stupid when it came to food. Once they found something to eat, they held on tight until they'd actually eaten it. That's what allowed Porter to catch so many out in the bay.

And that's how I'm going to catch this one.

He went back out into the aquarium hall and threaded the other end of the chain through the open front to the back of the metal cage before attaching it to the winch.

"What now?" the security guard said.

"Now we wait," Porter replied.

Come to daddy, you little fucker.

15

Stark and the team were in the air when the call came in.

"All units, Code Black. Forty, four, five North. Seventy-three, fifty-eight, twenty-three West. Passenger ferry in trouble. Clear out and take down if necessary."

"What's a Code Black?" Shona asked.

Stark waved her away. He talked into his own mouthpiece for several seconds.

The woman was insistent.

"Tell me," she said.

"Full scale terrorist alert. There's a ferry heading towards Manhattan, and they've lost contact with it. It's sailing blind, and on a collision course with Pier 8."

"What's the plan?"

"That's the easy part," he said. "I take a team aboard and check it out."

"And if it's them? The crabs?"

"Then we'll take them out."

Stark felt the old excitement rise.

Maybe I can finally get some payback.

He went up to the front of the chopper. The woman joined him. The view over Manhattan Island was stunning, but he had no time to take it in.

The pilot spoke.

"I have visual confirmation of the target. ETA five minutes."

And there, in the bottom left of a screen on the cockpit, there was a shot of the large red and white ferry.

At first there seemed nothing untoward… the ferry traveled on a straight course, heading for Manhattan. But as the chopper closed in, it became obvious… there were no people on deck. And the line it was on was straight.

Too straight.

"Take us in," Stark said. "Can you land?"

"Yes sir," the pilot replied. "It has two helipads - fore and aft."

In the bottom left of the screen Stark now had a clear view of the docks. Straight ahead was a pier and three ships at dock.

The ferry was heading straight for it.

Stark ordered the second chopper aft as the pilot brought the machine down on the fore helipad. Stark sent his team out under the rotors onto the deck.

"Wilkes... take two men and have a quick reconnoiter. Sergeant Brookes, are you there?"

"Here sir," a voice said from the second chopper.

"Check out the car bay. There may be people locked in their vehicles."

"What about me?" Shona Menzies said behind him.

"Stay aboard with the pilot. He'll look after you."

"I don't need..."

He stopped her.

"No time. Just stay here and keep your head down."

She didn't look happy.

But that's her problem at the moment. Not mine.

He took the remaining two men and headed for the ferry's bridge. He was thinking about the beach... in his mind's eye he could see the terrible sight of the children's father, *snipped* in half. It wasn't a huge leap of imagination from there to imagining a dark horde of the crabs flowing from the ferry.

"Wilkes? Anything?" he said.

"Give me a chance sir," the Lieutenant's voice said in his ear. "We just got here. All clear so far."

Stark led his men up the narrow stairs towards the ferry's bridge. It held no sign of life, nor any sign of a struggle. The power had stayed on... that much was obvious... but surely if anyone was still alive they would have been in contact?

The boat suddenly *lurched* to one side and came to an abrupt halt.

Amid the clamor of grinding metal and breaking glass Stark fell back to smash heavily against a door. His world went dim.

From nowhere he developed a thumper of a headache. Darkness had seeped in at the corners of his vision and the room hung from the sky at a strange angle. Only slowly did he become aware that someone shouted his name, and even that came from far away, like an out-of-tune radio.

"Stark. For Christ's sake Stark, come in. We've got a problem."

Wilkes?

"Come in Wilkes," he croaked into his mike. "I'm here."

"About time. Where have you been? And what happened?"

"I think we hit something."

He looked around. His team was getting groggily to their feet.

"Where are you?" he said.

"Deck 2, near the Casino. Pardon my French, but things are royally fucked up. I've got a man down, and crabs coming out of the woodwork."

The loud retort of gunfire started up, both in Stark's ear-piece and through the deck.

"Do you have an exit?"

"Negative. They've got us cornered."

"Hold on then. We're coming to you."

Stark's head rang, but at least he could function. So could his team. Apart from a few bruises, everyone gave the thumbs up. He led them out of the bridge.

"Sergeant Brookes. Please tell me you're okay," he said into his mike.

He heard the smile in the other officer's reply.

"All present and correct sir. But our chopper took a bashing. It's a dead duck. We're on our way to deck 2. ETA one minute."

The sound of small arms fire got suddenly louder and more insistent.

"Hold on Wilkes, we're coming in."

His ear-piece whistled as a new message came through.

Seems my head isn't the only thing that got damaged.

His chopper pilot's laconic drawl spoke in his ear.

"I don't want to spoil the party, but the General has ordered F12 deployment. There's a pair of Harriers on their way. You've got five minutes."

"Can you stall them?" Stark asked, but he already knew the answer… the CO and himself thought the same way.

"They're under strict radio silence sir... but I've been busy. There's a pair of pleasure boats heading your way. They'll stand off, but they're available if you need them for evac."

"Wilkes. Did you hear that?" Stark asked, but only got a burst of gunfire in reply. He started running, just as the screaming began.

16

Shona had only just recovered from being thrown around the chopper by the sudden jolt when she heard the pilot's conversation with Stark. She listened with mounting horror.

"You've got to stop them," she said. "You've still got men down there."

The pilot spoke softly in her ear.

"That's the job Miss," he said. "We know when we sign up that we are expendable."

Shona felt tears spring to her eyes. She went to the door of the chopper.

Hurry Stark. Please hurry.

Then she heard the screaming.

"Do something," she shouted to the pilot.

"I'm doing what I was told to do," the pilot said calmly. "Waiting."

"Well I'm under no such order," Shona said, and jumped down onto the deck.

17

Stark burst into the casino to be met with a wall of rampaging crustaceans.

They were packed in three-deep, a clacking, snapping frenzy. They clambered over and around each other as they tried to get to the three soldiers they had trapped behind a long bar.

A disco-ball light spun lazily overhead, giving the scene the semblance of a party in progress.

Wilkes and his men held their own, but had no way out through the press of crabs.

Crab shells cracked and split as the high-velocity bullets tore through them from close range, but still they came on, driven by their lust for meat.

"Wilkes. Have you got a flame thrower?" Stark said into his mike. He didn't hear the first reply as he moved quickly to avoid the lunging snap from a pincer. He took the claw off at the joint with a burst from his machine pistol.

"Say again Wilkes."

"We have a flame unit. Didn't want to use it unless as a last resort. In here it'll be as much danger to us as to them."

"Trust me," Stark said. "It's last resort time. Brookes. Are you there?"

The voice crackled in his ear.

"On the other side of the room from you sir. Flame units armed and ready."

"Then light them up. It's barbecue time."

The flame-thrower flared orange. The disco-ball sent fiery light flickering across their faces. In two seconds the place was burning, a thrashing hell full of screaming crabs searing flame and rolling smoke.

18

Immediately after she put her feet on the deck Shona realized just how stupid she was being.

The screaming and the gunfire continued loudly in her earpiece.

I have no weapon. I'll be no use to them.

Just as she turned to jump back into the chopper she heard a loud tearing, a *screech* of bending metal. The deck *thrummed* slightly underfoot. If she'd still been on the chopper she'd never have noticed.

Shona noticed that the ferry was drifting off the line it had been on.

She moved to the guardrail and looked over the side. A huge pincer snipped away at the hull of the boat from the inside. There was already a ten-foot tear in the metal that widened by the second.

That claw must be eight feet long!

The hull tore like paper and more of the crab emerged into daylight.

Shona started to shake, uncontrollably. The beast was *huge*. It looked ten feet and more across the shell, with claws nearly as long. The purple on the shell shone iridescent in the sunlight, shimmering alternately turquoise and black. The right pincer *clicked*, five times in quick succession as the crab pulled itself out into the water of the Bay. It started to move off, towards shore.

Shona watched, wide-eyed and trembling, as more crabs poured out of the hold; tens, no, hundreds of them, in sizes ranging from one to eight feet across the shell. They followed the large one in a line that led straight to the nearest pier. There they disappeared out of sight into the deep shadows under the pilings.

19

Wilkes appeared out of the melee in the casino dragging an injured soldier under the arms. The third man covered them. He stood between them and the crabs, wielding a flame-thrower to devastating effect, creating a wall as crabs struggled to escape the flame.

Stark's team moved instinctively to provide cover. Stark helped Wilkes with the injured man and together they got Wilkes' team under protection. They laid down a wall of flame and bullets. The crab attack paused, but they didn't retreat. They stood up high showing their bellies, pincers scraping the ceiling. One found the disco ball and crushed it to a mangled mass of metal and wiring, tossing it back towards the soldiers.

The air was suddenly filled with the noise of pincers clicking, like manic castanets. The front crabs threw themselves forward.

Stark shouted into his mouthpiece.

"Brookes. Get out of there now. Immediate retreat. We'll meet you up top. Double time."

"On our way," the reply crackled.

"Pilot? You there?" he asked.

"Here sir."

"Prepare for immediate evac. We have a man down."

The trooper with the flame-thrower set up an impenetrable barrier of fire behind them as the squad retreated at speed down the corridors.

The flames ate at the carpet, the walls and the ceiling, filling the enclosed space as fast as the soldiers could travel. They were soon running through a tunnel of choking, searing smoke and flame. Stark and his team shot out of the corridor like a bullet from a gun, smoke and flame following them onto the deck.

Brookes and his team were already there. Stark passed over the injured man.

"Get to the chopper. Wilkes, you're with me. Backup duty."

Behind Brookes' team he saw Shona Menzies leaning over the guardrail, her face ashen and drawn,

"And get her on board," he shouted. "We don't have time for babysitting."

Brookes saluted and left at a run after his men. Stark saw him bundle Menzies into the chopper.

Stark and Wilkes covered the corridor.

"Maybe we should have kept one of the flame-throwers," Wilkes said.

"I'd been thinking the same myself," Stark replied. They had to move back away from the building heat. "Be ready to run," he said.

But no crabs came out of the inferno.

Burn you bastards. Burn in hell.

Above the noise of the fire came the *whop-whop* of the chopper taking off.

"We're in the air," the pilot said seconds later. "Hold tight. I'll be right back."

"Negative," Stark said, staring at a growing speck in the northern sky. "No time for that. Get clear. We'll find our own way."

As he said it a large crab scuttled out of the corridor. Heat radiated from it, steam rising from the joints where the legs emerged from the shell. A pincer *snapped* and Stark had to roll quickly away. At the same instant Wilkes' weapon rattled into action. Stark rose just in time to see the crab implode and fall into a pile of hissing pieces of carapace.

He grabbed Wilkes and together they ran for the nearest railing.

They jumped simultaneously.

The air filled with the screeching whine of the approaching fighter.

Stark hit the water hard but managed to get to the surface with little difficulty. He turned on his back and looked up just as twin rocket trails flew from under the Harrier's wings.

They hit mid-ships and the whole middle section of the ferry went up with a *whoosh*.

Stark and Wilkes swam away. A small boat came up beside them and they heaved themselves aboard gratefully. They were just in time to see the chopper land on the pier.

"Well Colonel," Wilkes said. "Looks like a job well done."

The rest of the ferry blew without warning, sending debris hundreds of feet skywards. The explosion sent the blazing ruin drifting against the nearest boat in the dockyard. A secondary explosion blew the side out of the ferry. It collapsed with a screech of tearing metal.

In seconds a raging inferno was all that remained. A plume of black smoke rose high in the air as the first of many sirens sounded in the distance.

20

Newman had reluctantly shut down the Zoo for the day. Over the period of an hour the place went quiet.

Newman came back one last time to check on them.

“I hope you know what you’re doing Mr. Porter.”

Porter smiled.

“You can always stay and watch if you’d prefer?”

He took some small joy at seeing the fear that danced in Newman’s eyes as he backed away.

“Just fetch it back alive,” Newman said. By this time he was walking so fast out of the aquarium as to be almost running. “No live beast, no payment.”

I ain’t about to forget that in a hurry.

Soon there was only Porter and the young security guard left in the large echoing hall. Porter was amused to see that the youngster had armed himself with a pump-action shotgun. He held it gingerly, as if afraid it might go off at any second.

“I hope you ain’t planning to use that,” Porter said. “Your boss wants the creature alive. He plans to charge fifty bucks a time to see the fucker.”

The guard, Garston according to the tag on his shirt, kept his gaze fixed on the darkness on the far side of the octopus tank.

“That pecker-wood don’t know shit from shinola.”

Porter laughed loudly, the noise echoing around them.

“We can agree on *that* at least son. You got any smokes on you Garston?”

The security guard looked around.

“I’m on duty,” he said.

“Well hell lad,” Porter replied. “I ain’t gonna tell no one.”

Garston passed over a Marlboro, old-style full strength. Porter accepted a light and sucked smoke greedily, letting the familiar tang seep inside and ease him.

He’d hardly had time to think since arriving at the Zoo, but now that he was *crabbing* he started to feel a lot calmer.

"How long will we have to wait?" Garston said. His arms trembled with the weight of the gun and the barrel wavered alarmingly. Porter took the weapon from him and placed it on top of the steel cage.

"It takes as long as it takes lad," Porter said. "Sometimes they'll nab it straight away. Other days you get a whole pile of nothing."

"So what do we do?"

"We wait."

Silence fell as they smoked down the cigarettes.

There was a *whump* in the distance, and the muffled sound of sirens.

"What was that?" Garston said.

Porter shrugged.

"This is New York son. It could be fuckin' *anything.*"

From far off, somewhere way down behind the ruins of the octopus tank, came the noise that Porter was coming to recognize… the *clickity-click* of huge pincers.

21

Shona watched Stark and Wilkes climb out of the small boat and up the ladder onto the pier. She realized that she cared very much that they had survived.

Especially Stark.

She resisted the urge to hug them as they approached the chopper. Seconds later she was glad she had resisted; they stank. Even after their swim the smell of smoke hung strongly around them.

"Next time I tell you to stay in the chopper, please do as you're told," Stark said, smiling.

She smiled back, but it felt slightly forced as she remembered.

"We need to get under the pier," she said. "They went that way."

To his credit he knew immediately what she was talking about.

"How many of them?"

She was almost afraid to say.

Stark and Wilkes went quiet and still as she told them what she'd seen.

"What's under the pier?" she asked.

"Sewers, storage units, disused cargo trains… a couple of hundred years of messed up shit," Wilkes said.

"And we get to go play in it," Stark said wearily. "Get a team together, John. Gear up for close work in the tunnels. And make sure we've got plenty M-14s. You saw how much heat those suckers could take."

Wilkes nodded and left at a run.

"I'm coming with you on this one," Shona said.

Stark started to shake his head but she wasn't to be stopped.

"You need me. And you know it. You brought me in as the expert. Let me do my job."

"It's too dangerous," Stark said.

"For a *woman*?" she finished. "Don't you *dare* fucking patronise me."

Stark laughed.

"I was going to say... *for a civilian*. But you're right. We will need you in there. You'll find some *gear* in the chopper. Get suited up. I need to find a map of what we're headed into."

He was right about there being gear in the chopper. There was a whole wall of it. She was standing there looking bewildered when Wilkes came back. He laughed at the look on her face.

"Don't worry. *You* won't need all the combat kit. A pair of boots, a kevlar vest and you're sorted."

"I'll need a weapon," she said.

"No, you won't," Wilkes replied.

She smiled sweetly.

"Yes. I will. Don't worry, I won't shoot anyone. I've been around guns my whole life. Twelve bore shotguns mainly."

Wilkes laughed.

"We don't have a cannon for you. But can you handle a handgun?"

He handed her a pistol, a small Colt.

"It doesn't have much stopping power," she said. "Not against what we're after."

Again he laughed.

"If you think you're getting an assault rifle, you'll have a long wait. Without the training you'd be dangerous to everyone."

She reluctantly agreed with him, but the feel of the weight of the pistol as she holstered it felt somehow comforting. It was while putting the gun away that she remembered why they'd left the field station in the first place.

"The Park," she said. "We forgot about the crab sighting in the Park."

Wilkes stopped smiling.

"Sergeant Brookes and his team are on there way now. Let's hope they get there on time."

Stark returned as they were getting out of the chopper.

"Is the team ready?" he said.

Wilkes nodded.

"We've got eight men ready to roll on your order. Are we going in?"

Stark looked grim.

"I hope so. But it seems no one really knows what it's like in there. There's a man from the water utilities sending a map over but I don't know if it'll do us much good. We'll be going in mostly blind."

Wilkes nodded.

"Just like old times."

Stark managed a smile. He looked at Shona.

"Are you sure you want in?"

"No," she said. "But it's what you got me here for. When do we *roll*?"

"Five minutes. We can't afford to wait any longer."

Shona was very worried that they'd waited *far* too long already.

That fear was magnified when Stark led the team down the ladder that led under the pier. She was placed in the middle of the group, feeling small and a little fragile among so much muscle and weaponry.

"You know guys," she said, as she was about to step onto the ladder. "We could always just take off and nuke the site from orbit. It's the only way to be sure."

That got her a few laughs, and it started to settle the nerves that threatened to overwhelm her. But they came flooding back as she went down the ladder. Wilkes helped her off at the bottom and led her to the dark mouth of what looked like an old warehouse. He handed her a headband with a light and an ear-piece on it.

"We'll need these."

Stark was already leading the first of the men into the opening as she switched on the light. He put up a hand and clenched his fist. The men stopped.

There was a noise in the darkness beyond, a high squealing.

No crab ever made that sound.

Another noise joined the squealing; scurrying, like a thousand tiny feet on concrete. The men tensed, raising their weapons.

They rolled out of the dark.

Rats.

Thousands of rodents were tightly packed into a single squirming mass. The soldiers stepped back but the rats ignored them, tumbling en-masse into the water and swimming off strongly.

Stark looked on, bemused.

"Deserting a sinking ship?" he said.

Shona nodded.

"Something like that," she replied. "Although more likely they are fleeing a predator bigger and more vicious than they are."

One of the soldiers laughed nervously.

"More vicious that a New York sewer rat? I really don't want to meet that beast."

No, you don't. But that's where we're headed.

Shona followed as Stark led the way into the dark warehouse.

22

Porter and Garston smoked another of the younger man's cigarettes. Garston never took his eyes from the darkness beyond the smashed tank.

"What do we do if it comes back?"

Porter laughed.

"We catch it in this here cage and sell it to Newman. There's a hundred bucks in it for you if you help me."

Garston giggled. It sounded like the terrified laugh of a child.

Porter was just about to remark on it when he heard noises from deep in the bowels behind the tank.

Click, click.

The noise of the pincers was accompanied by high squeals. Porter knew that noise equally as well. He often had rats out at the cabin. A couple of years back he'd kept an old cat that was the most bad-tempered sonofabitch he'd ever seen. It used to catch the rats by the scruff of the neck and play with them until they squealed.

Down in the darkness the noise came again.

Just like that.

The chain jerked along its length.

"Get ready," Porter whispered. "Something's coming."

Something came… but it wasn't the crab. A furry brown carpet scurried up from below and spilled out from the octopus tank -- hundreds of them, squealing and jostling as they ran.

Something's got them spooked.

And it wasn't just the rats that were nervous. Garston picked up the shotgun and fired. Pieces of rat flew in a pink haze. They didn't slow as they ran over the men's feet.

Garston screamed and started to stamp his feet. His cigarette dropped from his mouth and hit a rat on the back. Fur sizzled and the rat squealed. Garston raised the shotgun again.

Porter put his hand on the barrel.

"Steady lad," he said. "They're just trying to escape. It'll be over in a second."

The rats kept coming, but soon started to thin in numbers. Far along the corridor a woman's voice rose in a high shriek as the carpet moved off en-masse. Porter and Garston were left alone once more.

The younger man shook violently. Porter carefully took the gun from him.

"Best I look after this for a while lad," he said.

Garston didn't complain. He lit up another cigarette and sucked at it greedily while Porter walked over towards the broken tank.

This isn't working. Fucker is too smart to fall for it.

He turned back to the youth.

"We're going to have to go in after it."

Garston laughed shakily.

"What's this we shit? This is your job."

Porter looked at the cage, then over into the darkness beyond the tank.

I can't carry it down there myself.

"I'll double my offer," he said. "Two hundred bucks if you give me a hand."

The youth's laugh got louder.

"Mister, I'll pay you two hundred bucks if you just let me get out of here."

Porter looked at the shotgun and considered making the kid an *offer he couldn't refuse.* But the kid looked *so* near to tears of fear, and so *young*, that he didn't have the heart for it.

"Look kid," Porter said softly. "I need to get that cage down to the lower levels. And I can't do it myself. How much will it take to get you to give me a hand?"

"How about half of what you're getting?"

It was Porter's turn to laugh.

"How about I attach *you* to the end of the chain and use you as bait?"

The youth looked into the darkness. He chewed on the cigarette a while before replying.

"Make it a thou' and I'll help you lug the cage down to the basement," he said. But I ain't going to be hanging around down there."

"In that case, I'll make it five hundred," Porter replied. He leaned over and began to drag the cage across the floor. "Grab the winch. We're going to need it."

Garston looked to the far side of the room, then down into the blackness past the tank.

"Five hundred?" he said.

Porter nodded.

"Cash in hand, soon as I get paid."

Garston picked up the winch and helped Porter manhandle the cage across the wet floor of the octopus tank. He stopped as they approached the dark maw that led down to the bowels.

"Five hundred," Porter said softly. "Just keep telling yourself that."

They got the cage through to the far side. Porter waited for his eyes to adjust to the gloom and looked around. They stood in a cramped area, no more than eight feet wide, running along the back of all the aquarium tanks. The far wall from them opened out into another chamber beyond, one that echoed the noise of the dragging chain back at them.

"Where does that go?" Porter asked.

Garston had gone pale again.

"To the basement," the lad said. "But there are tunnels down there that go way down deep, to the subway and beyond."

Porter started to drag the cage in that direction.

"Come on then lad. The deal was that we got this here cage to the basement."

"There's rats down there," Garston said.

Porter laughed, the noise echoing around them, making him sound like a cheap horror movie villain.

"Not any more there ain't son. Now come on. The sooner it's done the sooner you can get out of here."

Porter passed the shotgun back to the youth. He placed it in a long holster under his left arm.

The youth took a look back to the lit aquarium hall, then bent to help Porter drag the cage. Together they went through into the chamber beyond, which was little more than a deep stairwell. Porter stood at the top and listened. There was no sound but their breathing.

They headed down.

23

It felt dank in the dark shadows under the pier, but it got colder still as Shona and the team entered the warehouse proper. It ran most of the length of the pier above them, but where the pier was a hive of activity, down here all was silent and still. The place was derelict, and by the looks of it had been so for a good number of years. Rotting crates lay piled against the wall, sunken and slumped like half-asleep drunks. The floor was damp, their lights reflecting shimmering patterns of colour where oil had been spilled. Their footsteps echoed. Dark shadows crept around them as their headlights probed along the walls and into corners.

They found nothing but more rotting crates. One of the soldiers poked at the side of one with the barrel of his gun. It fell in with an obscene moist sucking sound. A pile of mouldy something that might once have been curtains slithered out and fell at his feet. The remains of the crate collapsed in on itself with a clatter and the warehouse rang with the sound of cracking wood.

The soldier stood back, shame-faced.

The rest of them stood still, listening, waiting for any response to the sound. Shona was almost afraid to move. The men around her seemed tense.

They have good reason to be.

Nothing moved. The team relaxed, if only slightly, and moved forward once more.

Stark stopped when they reached the end of the warehouse space. Light still seeped in here from the pilings of the pier, but ahead of them, where the pier ended and the edge of the city proper began, it was almost full blackness.

Stark held up three fingers and motioned forward. Wilkes took two men with him and headed ahead, their lights soon lost in the deeper gloom. Stark led the rest of them on. Shona heard Wilkes in her ear-piece.

"Nothing here but more junk sir. All clear."

They walked through a large doorway. Any doors that had once stood there had long since gone. The opening led into another large space, but one that had a lower ceiling. The walls here weren't concrete, they were red brick, and arched ten feet overhead in a cathedral-like vault. Archways led off on either side at regular intervals. A rusting steam locomotive sat at the far end of the vault, somewhat lopsided where it had partially been de-railed.

Wilkes and his two companions stood next to the derelict train, looking down at something on the ground.

"You'd better come on over," Wilkes said in her ear. "You'll need to see this."

I really don't.

She walked forward slowly, flanked by Stark and the rest of the men. As she reached Wilkes she looked down. The beam from her headlight alighted on a scene from a nightmare.

Two bodies lay next to one of the locomotive's wheels. Or rather, bits of two bodies lay there. The white bone of a rib-cage showed through the remains of a coat; the nub of a thighbone showed where a leg had been taken off… a leg of which there was no sign. Two fingers lay side by side, dried and shrivelled like old sausages. The more she looked, the more she saw. Body parts were strewn over a wide area, the pieces showing signs of having been snipped apart, almost clinically. Dried blood had soaked into the packed earth on the ground.

Wait a minute. That's not right.

She bent and touched her fingers to the ground.

Dry.

Her heart sank to the pit of her stomach.

"Street people do you think?" Stark asked. "Caught here when the crabs came in?"

Shona took her time before replying.

"Caught here, certainly," she said. "But not today."

Stark bent closer to look at the bodies. When he stood his face looked grim. And worried.

"I see what you mean. How long ago do you think? Two months?"

Shona nodded.

"About that. The crabs have been here longer than we expected."

"That's not possible," Stark said, but he had gone visibly paler.

"With these beasts, nothing is impossible," she replied.

Stark stood away from the bodies.

"Okay," he said to Shona. "You're the expert. If these things have been under Manhattan for months, where will they be?"

She didn't have to take too long to think on her answer.

"They'll be deep, where it's dark and damp. They're natural burrowers and tunnellers."

"Then they could be anywhere down here," Stark whispered.

That's what I'm afraid of. And we've no idea how many of them there might be.

The side passages looked darker and deeper than before as the team moved out. Shona lagged slightly behind, looking back at the bodies.

Two months.

Maybe more.

And in the height of the breeding season.

I think we're in trouble.

24

Porter and Garston lugged the cage and the winch down four flights, down a stairwell that got steadily dimmer.

"Is there any lighting at all down here?" Porter asked.

Garston had started to look worried; getting more agitated with each new flight of stairs.

"There are only emergency lights in the basement itself," he said. "Hardly anyone ever goes down there. Below that? Who knows? There are passages that lead to the sewers then the subway and all kinds of mixed up shit down there."

Porter stopped for a rest on the next landing.

"How much further to the basement?" he asked.

Garston looked over the railing.

"Three more flights. After that, I'm gone, and you owe me five hundred."

Porter smiled.

"I guess you can afford to give me another cigarette then?" he said.

Garston almost laughed as he handed over the carton.

They both lit up.

Garston looked over the railing again.

"Do you really think you have a chance of catching this thing?"

"Son," Porter said as he exhaled a lung-full of smoke. "I'm the best damned crabber on the Long Island shore. Hell, maybe even the best on the whole Eastern Seaboard. If *anybody* is going to catch that thing, it's me."

While they smoked Porter listened for any sounds from below. Pipes gurgled, and once he heard the far-off sound of running machinery. But there was nothing to suggest that the crab was anywhere close.

He knew that didn't mean anything.

Sneaky little fucker could be anywhere.

He decided to give Garston one more try.

"I'll double the money if you stay and help me catch it," he said.

Garston smiled ruefully.

"Five hundred guaranteed, with me free and clear and out in the daylight in ten minutes, is worth a lot more than a thou' I might get too dead to see."

They finished the cigarettes and hefted the cage and gear. After relaxing, just slightly, during the smoke, Garston showed signs of spreading panic. He started to talk, faster and faster.

"Five hundred bucks will come in handy," Garston said. "I've got a girl. She wants to go to Florida for a weekend. You ever been to Florida?

He didn't wait for an answer.

Porter backed down onto a flat floor and realised they had reached the bottom. It was darker here, with deep shadows in the corners. The only light shone above a swing door and a sign that read *Sub-Basement 3 – No Unauthorised Admission.*

Porter moved in that direction, away from the stairs.

Garston was still talking.

"They done got this beach that goes on forever, the sand so yellow it hurts your eyes. And they have these broads that parade up and down with their tits hanging out. My girl doesn't know that. She's just seen Miami on the television and thinks it would be cool to hang out there. I…"

Snick.

The cage dropped to one side with a clang and clatter. At first Porter thought that Garston had tripped.

Then he saw the claw.

The crab had been hiding underneath the metal stairs. Just as Garston reached the bottom it reached out between steps and took his left foot off just above the ankle.

Garston lay against the corridor wall, staring at the stump. His foot still sat on the stairs. The spray of blood covered a large triangular area. It still spurted, an almost three foot arc that steamed in the air. The youth, even paler now, looked on, aghast. Porter knew that the pain hadn't hit yet.

But it will.

He didn't have time to help the youth. The crab scuttled out from the gap under the stairs. It snapped its claws together.

Clickety-click.

Standing up on its legs it showed Porter its belly. Down here in the cramped area it looked even bigger than before.

Porter shuffled to one side, putting the cage between him and the crab. The crab barely slowed. It came forward, snapping. Porter bent, trying to reach the length of chain, anything that could help as a weapon. But the cage itself was in the way.

And the crab is too close.

The creature *snipped* at the cage. The metal didn't give. But it did bend. The right claw grabbed tight at the roof of the cage and *pulled.* Porter grabbed the edge and tried to pull against it, but the crab proved to be incredibly strong. It dragged the cage to one side and threw it aside, the noise as it hit the wall almost deafening.

But not as loud as the shotgun blast. Something *tugged* at the cloth of Porter's jacket. But the bulk of the shot hit the crab's shell. Pieces of carapace flew. But the shell withstood the blast. No real damage had been done.

It had however drawn the beast's attention back to Garston. That gave Porter time to bend and lift the chain. He had no real plan in mind, apart from getting the crab to take the eel bait that still hung at the end.

Garston had other ideas. He raised the shotgun again.

"Don't kill it," Porter shouted.

"Fuck that," Garston shouted back. Porter ducked just in time as the gun boomed.

He was showered in small pieces of shell, and he smelled the unmistakable whiff of crabmeat.

The bastard has killed it.

But when he looked up it was to see the crab scuttle away through the swing doors. One of its legs lay on the ground at Porter's feet. Porter kicked it to one side and ran over to kneel by Garston.

The lad was as white as a sheet, his eyelids fluttering. The blood still flowed at the stump, but it was barely a trickle.

The poor bastard is nearly gone.

Even as Porter knelt at his side, the lad's head lolled to one side and he let out one last drawn out gasp. Then he was gone.

Porter looked back up the stairs, then at the swing doors.

Fifty thou'. Remember the fifty thou'.

He rolled the long chain into a loop and draped it over his shoulders. He didn't want to, but he forced himself to go through Garston's pockets. He found a packet of cartridges for the shotgun, a fresh pack of cigarettes and a lighter. He put them all in his jacket, and took the shotgun from the holster. Without looking back he headed through the doors into the darkness.

25

The first passageway Shona and the team tried proved to be a dead-end after only thirty yards. The red brick arch crumbled in places, and long strands of pale lichen and roots hung limply, slapping against Shona's face as she tried to peer into the corners.

There was little sign that the space had been used apart from a pair of rotting sleeping bags and a small pile of fast food cartons.

Wilkes prodded one of the sleeping bags.

"This could be the *home* of the ones who…"

He didn't have to finish. They all knew what he meant. Shona thought it would be a long time before she forgot the sight of those two pitiful fingers lying on the dirt.

Stark came to Shona's side.

"What do you think?" he said.

"There's no way they came through here," she replied.

Stark nodded, agreeing.

"Let's move on. We've got a lot of ground to cover.

Stark lifted a finger to his ear and did something with his headset.

"Alpha team reporting," he said. "We're going in deeper."

"Reporting in?" Shona asked. "We can do that down here?"

"For now," Stark said. "While we're near the surface. If we get deeper then it's less likely."

"And backup?" Shona asked. "Do we have any?"

Stark smiled grimly.

"Well, there's Sergeant Brookes' team. But they're halfway across Manhattan in Central Park. Let's hope we don't have to walk that far."

Let's hope.

Stark led the team out again.

The second passageway proved more hopeful as a lead. It opened out slightly into a wide tunnel that led away from the sea in a very slight down slope. A corroded set of rails showed where a cargo train had once ran. Whispers ran and echoed around them. Their headlights showed more of the red-brick arch above. This one was clear of the damp and hanging roots. Indeed some of the brickwork looked almost new. Shona tried to look further down the tunnel but her light could not pierce more than twenty yards ahead in the gloom.

When she started to turn towards Stark something caught her eye. She knelt and checked the ground at their feet. Lieutenant Wilkes stepped forward but she waved him back.

"Wait. There are some tracks here."

She bent closer. Her first instincts had been right.

Crab tracks. Big ones. And lots of them.

"They came this way?" Stark asked.

"It certainly looks like it."

She was aware that around her the men stiffened, and became a lot more watchful as they headed deeper into the tunnel.

It got cold quickly. The air tasted slightly metallic. Shona heard, as if from far off, an intermittent rumbling noise. Wilkes saw her looking up.

"Traffic noise," he said. "We're off the docks and under Manhattan itself by now."

"It's hard to believe all this is underfoot and no one ever thinks about it," she said.

Wilkes laughed.

"You ain't seen nothing yet," he said. "There a whole other city down here. I hope you're prepared for a walk. We could be down here a while."

The tunnel led steadily down for a hundred yards before Stark brought the men to a halt.

"Miss Menzies," he said. "You need to see this.

She looked to where he indicated. Three pyramidal piles, each almost two feet high, sat in the centre of the tunnel. In the light from the head-lights it showed up grey, almost ghostly.

"Is this what I think it is?" Stark asked.

She nodded.

"Crab scat. And a lot of it."

She knelt.

"It's old," she said and plunged a hand deep into the nearest pile, ignoring the groans and complaints from the men around her.

"You can tell a lot from crab scat," she said.

Wilkes laughed loudly.

"I think I already know *all* I want to."

She pulled a fistful of damp material from the centre of the pile and studied it closely. She ran some of it between her fingers. It fell to the ground slowly, little more than fine dust.

Two, maybe three months. It fits with what we saw earlier.

Stark came forward.

"Anything?"

She was about to reply when she found a more solid piece. She blew away the dusty detritus around it, and gasped.

"What?" Stark said. "What is it?"

She held it up and showed him. She had uncovered a human fingernail, cracked and broken, but unmistakable.

"There's no possible doubt about it now. The things we are after don't *just slice and dice*. They are man-eaters."

26

Porter had to stand in the gloom beyond the swing doors for several minutes before his eyes adjusted to the near-dark. Black shadows hung everywhere he looked, and vague shapes were scattered around on the floor of the room he'd entered. After a while they began to resolve into tables, chairs and piles of old filing cabinets, some of which were metal, some older still… huge solid wooden constructions that would take a team of workmen to lift.

There was no sign of the crab.

Porter took out the shotgun and loaded it by feel. He stood still and listened. The only sound was the far off rumbling of machinery that he guessed, given how far down they'd come, to be some part of the subway system.

I have to get the little fucker's attention soon. I ain't going crawling around in no dark tunnels on his account.

Once he started to move he was able to pick his way though the debris easily enough. He took it slowly and carefully, aware that at any second he could hear the *snick* that would spell his death.

He was grateful for the feel and solidity of the gun in his hands. After seeing the effect the shot had, he was confident he could at least fend off an all out attack. But that wasn't the plan. The length of chain weighed heavy on his shoulders, but there was no way he was going to ditch it. He was here to go crabbing, to get the catch of his life.

But first I have to find the fucker.

He moved deeper into the gloom. The further in he got, the more he could hear of the deep rumbling. At the far end of the basement he found another stairwell, dark, dank and uninviting. The rumbling was louder down there, and a dim light showed several flights below.

Porter did a quick sweep of the room he was in. He couldn't see anywhere else that the crab could have gone.

But I don't want to be poking around any further than I have to.

He took out a cigarette and lit up. The flare from the lighter blinded him momentarily, and he realised he'd just been really stupid. If the attack came now, he was defenceless. He held his breath, listening to his heart pounding in his ears, trying to hold the shotgun steady despite sudden tremors in his hands.

There was no *snick.*

By the time he was able to see properly he had his composure back. He smoked the cigarette down to the butt before looking down the stairwell again. The darkness hadn't got any more inviting.

Fuck it. Nothing ventured, nothing gained.

He started down. Once on the stairs he could feel the rumbling as a vibration through the soles of his feet. It was almost enough to make him give up. But the thought of the money was more important than any fear he had for his own safety.

He kept going.

It got steadily lighter. At the bottom of the stairs he emerged into a narrow tunnel. Ten yards further this opened out onto a set of subway tracks lit every twenty yards with a bright lamp.

Porter's heart sank.

It could be anywhere by now.

Then he heard it, loud even above the distant rumbling of a train.

Click, click, clickety click.

He had broken into a run even before the screams followed close behind.

The screams turned into full-blown shrieks as he came out of the tunnel into a dim cavernous area that had once been a station. A group of heavily swaddled people ran along the platform, coming straight towards him. Behind them there was a white flash.

Snick.

The crab was there, its white claws looking almost iridescent as they flashed left and right. Blood spurted in a high arc. More screams followed.

Porter had to stand to one side as the swaddled mass of people pushed past him into the tunnel. One of them stopped. He couldn't tell whether it was a man or a woman… the face was covered in a thick layer dust and grime.

"Get out of here man. They've found us."

Before Porter had time to reply the people had all pushed past him. He heard their footsteps echoing away down the corridor but by then his attention was on the crab.

The loss of a leg hadn't slowed it down any. It stood over two bodies, slashing and cutting. The pincers fed strips of bleeding meat into a maw already red and dripping.

I guess the eel wasn't tempting enough.

Porter pulled himself up onto the platform. The chain scratched loudly against the concrete. The crab lifted its eyes, two pearly globs on long stalks that swivelled to stare straight at him.

"That's right fucker," Porter said. "Daddy's here."

He had little idea what he could feasibly do next. He had a vague idea that involved crippling the beast enough that he could drag it back up top. That had sounded fine in his head, but here in the gloom of the disused station it now seemed completely impractical.

But it's all I've got.

He walked towards the crab. Every nerve in his body was telling him to run the other way, and his bowels were so loose he might well need a cork. But he didn't trust himself with the shotgun at distance. He'd have to get up close and personal to have any chance at all.

The crab watched him come forward. Almost casually it tore a long length of flesh from a human leg and fed it, inch by inch, into its mouth.

As Porter got within fifteen yards it stood upright and showed him its belly.

Clickity click.

It snapped its pincers in the air and scurried forward, straight at Porter. He raised the gun and took aim. But before he had time to pull the trigger the beast veered sharply to its left and slid from the platform onto the rails.

Oh no you don't.

Porter ran to the edge.

The crab was already heading off at speed further down the tunnel, deeper into the subway system. All that he could see was the white flashes of its pincers reflecting the light from the track-side lamps but all too quickly it was lost in the distance.

It doesn't like the gun. Little fucker learned fast.

That gave Porter hope that he might have an edge that would help him catch the crab. He jumped down onto the rails and, as fast as he was able, followed the crab into the tunnel system.

27

Stark brought the team to an abrupt halt. They'd been following the large tunnel for nearly fifteen minutes, with no noise but the distant rumbling of traffic above them. Their easy walk came to an end at a junction. The way ahead had been blocked by a pile-up of wrecked carriages and steam engines, rusting heaps all jammed tightly together in the main passageway. Two men went forward and studied the wrecks. One turned and gave Stark a thumb's down.

"No way through that way sir."

Shona knew what was coming next as Stark turned to her.

"So, left or right?" he asked.

I don't know. I'm new here.

She walked to the left tunnel. A warm draft of air wafted against her face and she smelled fish. The right tunnel sloped downward at a steeper angle. The brickwork was older, some of it crumbling, and the air felt cold and damp.

She wanted to say *left* and take the easy option.

But I've seen these crabs. And if they get loose in the city, there will be havoc. We have to find them. And find them quick.

"This one," she said to Stark. "We should head down here."

Stark didn't question her judgement. He moved the team out.

The way became more difficult almost immediately. The ground underfoot felt soft, almost slimy. Thick sticky ooze sucked at their boots and they struggled to stop sliding and slipping. Overhead on the arch the brick showed signs of decay, gaps and holes in places. Ghost white roots hung limply, wafting in the slight breeze. The tunnel was noticeably narrower than the one they'd been in previously, being only ten feet or so at the widest.

But they were heading in the right direction. Fresh tracks showed in the clay-like ooze ahead of them, unmistakable signs of crab movement.

From what she could see all the tracks led in the same downward direction. There was no indication that the beasts had ever came up this passage, and that in itself was puzzling Shona. She was so far lost in thought that she walked into the back of Lieutenant Wilkes who had stopped in front of her.

A row of four team members stood looking at a large gaping hole in the side of the tunnel. It was six feet wide and led sharply downwards into deep blackness. Stark motioned Shona over.

“This doesn’t look man-made to me,” he said. “It looks like it’s been *dug*.”

After a glance Shona agreed. Pieces of brick lay strewn around the area, and a large mound of mud had been deposited to one side.

“I told you they were burrowers,” she said. “Some of them… some of the smaller ones, went this way. But most of the ones I saw leaving the ferry were too big for this hole.”

She saw several of the men look up at that remark, and smile, disbelieving.

They didn’t see the beasts. I did.

“But if they’re tunnelling, they could be anywhere,” she said to Stark. “You’re going to need more manpower, more search parties.”

He looked grim.

“I’ve had a hard enough time as it is getting this team together,” he said. “I need proof to take back.”

“But the ferry…” Shona began.

Wilkes butted it.

“The ferry was totally burned out Miss,” he said. “All we have in the way of proof is a couple of bits of shell. The brass are hardly going to evacuate Manhattan on *that* evidence.”

“Then they’re even more stupid than I thought,” Shona said indignantly.

Wilkes laughed.

“*Now* you’re getting the idea.”

Stark brought Shona back to the situation at hand.

"So, do we go down there?" he said, and pointed at the hole in the passageway.

She shook her head.

"No. We need to follow the main group. We need to know what they're up to."

Before it's too late.

She didn't say it, but she knew by the look on Stark's face she didn't have to.

Stark led the men out again. Wilkes led Shona away from the hole.

"Any theories Professor?" Wilkes asked, smiling.

"Too many," she replied. "That's the problem. Until we find them, we won't know what they're up to."

Wilkes laughed again.

"And when we do find them, we *will* know what they're up to. But my bet is we're not going to like it."

"And I'd say the odds are on your side on that one."

They caught up with the rest of the team and kept going down the passage.

"Any idea where this goes?" she asked Wilkes.

He shook his head.

"No. But I know there are some that run for forty miles and more up into the hills. Either that, or we'll come to a sewer or subway tunnel. Folks have been tunnelling and building down here for centuries now."

And now it's not just people.

Shona's mood was getting increasingly bleak the further down they went. Wilkes had noticed and tried to lift the mood with a series of bawdy anecdotes about life in the forces, but she only had half an ear on it. Mostly she was listening for the noise she knew would come eventually, and she wasn't surprised when she heard it.

Click click clickity click.

What did surprise her was where the noise came from. It came from behind them, back up the tunnel.

"Stark!" she said.

"I heard it," he replied.

He deployed the men in two ranks of four. They stood, guns at the ready, as the noise came closer. The *clicking* echoed and rang in the confined space, sounding like a manic drummer hitting a tin can.

Oh my god. There are hundreds of them.

They saw the eyes reflecting their head-lights first… many pairs of eyes, like fireflies on a summer's night. Coming slowly, almost ghosting into view, the white claws were next to show, waving and swaying in a macabre dance.

Shona's first thought had been near the mark. There were maybe a hundred crabs packed tight in the enclosed space, some even clambering over the backs of the others.

"Where the hell did these come from?" Wilkes asked.

"Look at the size of them," she said. "I think we've found what went down that hole back there."

The crabs were mostly between three and five feet across the back, with pincers the same length again. They came on remorselessly.

Stark let them come until the noise was almost deafening. The crabs, seeing the team ahead of them, scurried faster.

"Fire!" Stark shouted.

Even with her ears protected somewhat by the headset the noise rang like being inside a great bell. Muzzle flashes lit up the tunnel in a bright strobe. The crabs danced in time. Pieces of shell, leg and pincer flew in the air as armour-piercing rounds tore into the massed crabs. They kept coming, even the wounded ones

We're not doing enough damage.

"Fall back," Stark shouted. "Wilkes. Use the M14."

Shona moved as quickly as she could, sliding backwards with the rest of the men. They kept firing as they retreated, the air full of noise and smoke and muzzle-flash.

"Close your eyes," Wilkes said.

She turned towards him just as he pulled the tab on the incendiary.

"Fire in the hold," he called, and lobbed the grenade at the approaching crabs.

Shona didn't need to be told twice. She closed her eyes, but even through the lids the light *flared*, brighter than the noonday sun.

The blast almost blew her off her feet. It got hot… very hot. She was forcibly pulled away and when she opened her eyes she found that Stark had her in a hug.

"Sorry," he said, looking suddenly embarrassed. She pecked him on the cheek and disentangled herself. She turned back to look up the tunnel. She had to squint; the light was still too bright after the previous gloom in the tunnel.

All that was left of the crabs was a fused burning mess.

Smoke slowly cleared. She expected to see more crabs pressing behind. Instead the dust cleared to reveal that the tunnel had collapsed. Tons of brick and rubble had buried any beasts that had escaped the blast.

But it was no cause for celebration.

Their way back out was completely blocked.

28

Somehow Porter had got lost. He'd followed the crab as well as he'd been able; sometimes by sight of the white flashes of the pincers, other times by the sound of the *clickety-click*. And once he found a new pile of scat, still steaming in the cold air of the tunnel.

But for the past five minutes all he'd seen was tunnel, and all he'd heard was the distant rumble of trains.

Has it gone to ground?

The dark closed in further, with only every second or third light working. Porter slowed, then came to a halt.

Fuck this for a lark.

He leaned against the tunnel wall and lit up a smoke. He almost jumped out of his skin when someone spoke close to his ear.

"Hey Jim, can you spare one of those gaspers?"

There was a side tunnel to his left that he hadn't noticed; barely wide enough for someone to pass through. The swaddled figures that came out of it seemed barely human.

Mole-people.

He'd heard the rumours; of people who lived completely out sight of everyone else, scouring the depths for what little they could find to survive on.

Scavengers. Like the crabs.

There were three of them; pale, wide-eyed and thin to the point of emaciation. They stared at his cigarette as if it was worth a fortune. The one who'd spoken moved forward, but stopped when he saw the gun.

A laugh came from the decrepit bundle of clothes.

"Your pea-shooter won't stop them," he said.

Porter stopped in mid-puff.

Them?

"You've seen the crab then? Did it come this way in the last five minutes?"

The figures were still staring at the smoke. Porter sighed and took out the packet. He held out three cigarettes.

"The crab?" he asked. "Did it come this way this morning."

The one who spoke snatched the smokes from Porter's hand and passed them around before answering.

"Not today," he said. ""Ain't seen none for a week or so, but we've been keeping out of their way. Nasty buggers they are, all that *clicking* and *snapping*."

"And they ate Jennie. Ate her right up," another said, surprising Porter by having a woman's voice.

Porter felt a new chill settle in his bones.

"We *are* talking about crabs here, right?"

All three nodded.

"Huge bastards they are too. They started showing up last year in the lower tunnels. We don't know how many there are down there now; nobody who's gone to look has ever come back."

"How many have you seen?" Porter whispered.

"Since last year? More than a hundred. Maybe two hundred. Some as big as cows."

"Bigger," the female said. "It did this."

She struggled inside the layers of clothes and for a horrible second Porter thought she was going to disrobe completely. But when she brought out her arm, it was worse than he'd imagined. It had been taken off just above the elbow, and what was left was a suppurating stump, the flesh around it swollen, grey and *sweating*. She put it away.

"I was lucky," she said. "It was a little one. The one that ate Jennie only just got into the tunnel here."

Porter looked at the subway walls. At the point where they stood the tunnel was more than five metres wide.

He turned back to the *mole people*, but they had already slipped away, back into the darkness. He stuck his head into the cramped side tunnel, but it was full dark in there, and it stank, of acrid body odour and stale shit. He backed away fast.

Suddenly the idea of chasing around down here no longer appealed, and fifty thou' didn't seem nearly as enticing as it had previously.

I need help. I can always come back.

That's how he rationalised it to himself, but the feeling he felt most as he headed back along the tunnels was a rising sense of panic.

That feeling got stronger as he came to a junction he did not remember ever passing on the way in. Both tunnels ahead of him headed downwards; damp, dimly-lit caverns.

Just the kind of place for crabs to be hiding.

He looked back the way he had come, but from here it looked just like any other tunnel. There was no doubt about it now. He was completely lost.

Clickety-click.

It came from back in the direction of the mole people.

But it was answered from the right hand tunnel ahead of him.

Then again.

And again, a cacophony of sound rising in waves from the cavern.

Porter turned to his left and moved into the tunnel. The *clickety-click* behind him got louder. He started to move faster. Soon he was almost running.

He ditched the heavy chain.

I won't need it.

I'm not the hunter any more.

I'm the hunted.

29

Shona watched three men work at the pile of rubble, trying to find a way back through. But even from twenty yards back she could see that the mass of stone that had fallen was too much for them to move.

It looks like a job that will take days. And that's time we don't have.

She walked over to Stark.

"We need to go down further," she said.

"Why? We found the crabs. We should get back and bring a clear-up team down here."

She shook her head.

"We found *some* crabs. But we haven't found the big ones. And we need to know where they are hiding."

Stark looked back at the rubble and sighed.

"There's no way out that way anyway. We need to get to somewhere where we can get out a message. And right now the only way is down."

He called the men back from the rubble and after a brief check of all the team's ear-pieces and headlights, he once more led them out.

They moved slower now, more careful, aware of every sound, every movement around them. The further down they travelled the older and more decrepit the brickwork became. Thin grey tendrils wafted above them and everything felt damp and humid. Ooze sucked at their boots.

No one spoke, but Shona sensed an air of tension, possibly even of desperation, that had not been there before.

"GPS has gone offline sir," she heard Wilkes say.

That's it. We're off the grid, without a map.

The tunnel kept its downward trajectory. Once the whole place shook and dust fell around them as something barrelled past, seemingly just beyond the wall.

"Maybe we could break through?" Shona asked Stark as the vibration receded. "Sounds like the subway is just through there."

He shook his head.

"If the crabs are contained in here, then it would be madness to give them another way out. Especially into a populated area. No. We keep going. This has to lead somewhere."

He was proved right five minutes later.

They heard it before they reached it, a rumble, like distant thunder. It got much louder as the passageway opened out into a huge sewer hub. Six different tunnels fed into a canal that flowed off and away down a wide culvert across the chamber from them. The whole place was a marvel of brickwork, high vaulted archways and the roaring of water. Light came in from somewhere above, dancing in the shadows. A pathway led, via a series of iron steps and railings, all the way round the circle, a diameter of nearly twenty metres. From where she stood Shona saw a ladder about a third of the way round that led up towards where the light came in. She was about to step forward when Stark pulled her back.

He put a finger to his lips and pointed across the chamber.

At the mouth of the draining culvert two grey shapes sat, one closer than the other; a torrent of water flowing smoothly over their streamlined shape. She'd taken them for stone, possibly concrete reinforcements. But when she looked closer she could see the ghost-white claws, just below the surface, wafting to and fro in the current, sampling and tasting.

My god. They're ten feet across.

At least.

The team backed off, retreating up the tunnel.

"You saw?" Stark asked her when they were twenty yards back.

She nodded.

"Will they attack?"

Crabs are all different; some passive, some naturally aggressive. But everything she'd seen so far led to just one conclusion.

"Yes. At the slightest provocation."

Stark pursed his lips.

“Yet we have to get out of here. We need to try for that ladder.”

Wilkes stepped forward. He had a grenade in his hand.

“Shall we use the M-14 again sir?”

Stark shook his head.

“Too risky. We don’t want to bring half of Manhattan down on top of us. And if the blast went up, there’s no telling if we’d have civilian casualties above us. No. Stealth is our best option here. We’ll try to get round the chamber and up the ladder, and hope they pay us no mind.”

Hope is generally not a good idea when faced with a force of nature.

But Shona didn’t say it.

Wilkes led the team out again. There were four men in front of her as they started to walk, slowly, around the perimeter of the cavern.

Shona couldn’t take her eyes off the crabs. They seemed to be feeding. She didn’t let herself dwell too long on *what* they were feeding on. This was Manhattan. It could be anything. But whatever they were eating, at least it kept their attention away from the team.

They shuffled around the narrow footpath, forced to move in single file. Wilkes was first to reach the small platform at the base of the iron ladder. He looked up, and Shona followed his gaze.

Light came in from a hundred feet overhead, from what looked to be a large grate of some kind. For all she knew it could be one of the main roads, but no traffic noise would be discernible above the roar of the water around them. The team crowded around on the platform. There was just enough room for all of them.

Wilkes put a hand on the ladder. The first rung fell to powder in his hand, little more than a pile of rust. He reached up higher. The next rung up was sturdier but still split in two with a load creak that had them all holding their breath. The crabs kept feeding.

The Lieutenant reached up, almost on tip-toe. He put all his weight on the third rung. It held. He tugged, hard. Still it held. He holstered his weapon and hauled himself up, feet dangling just off the ground. Hand over hand he pulled himself up to the next rung, then three more after that. He turned back when his feet were almost level with Shona's eyes and gave a thumbs-up. He scampered up further. Craning her neck Shona saw him pull himself into another tunnel some twelve feet up. He turned and waved.

"Okay," Stark said, leaning close to Shona's ear. "You next. Can you get up there?"

In truth, she wasn't sure she had the arm strength.

But I'm not about to admit it.

"Boost me up," she said. She noticed a slight delay before he put his arms at her waist and lifted her up to the first steady rung.

It proved easier than she'd thought. After four rungs she was able to get a foothold and scamper quickly up to join Wilkes. She let him pull her into the side tunnel and turned back.

She was just in time to see the nearest crab raise itself out of the water and look straight at the members of the team. It raised its pincers and clacked them together, the noise audible above the rush of water.

The second crab brought its head up. It too clacked.

Down below she saw Stark boost the next man onto the ladder.

"Hurry!" she called.

But there would not be time to get all the men up. The nearest crab had already hauled itself up to its full height, almost filling the culvert.

It scuttled forward.

"Fire!" Stark called.

The tunnel was filled with the thunderous roar of gunfire and the lightning flash from muzzles.

30

Porter ran down the subway tunnel, aware that a train might slam towards him at any second. He could hear little above his own heavy breathing and the thudding of blood in his ears, but he was afraid to turn and look back.

My imagination is doing enough of that already.

In his mind's eye he saw a horde of clacking pincers just inches from his heels. That, and the image of the bleeding stump that had killed the security guard was enough to give him impetus.

There was a side tunnel ahead to his left… a narrower opening just wide enough for one person to move through.

The fuckers won't get in there.

He threw himself inside. Within five yards it was nearly pitch black, only a dim grey light coming in from behind him, and his body was blocking most of that. He stopped, and turned to face the opening.

All was quiet. Eventually his heart slowed and his breathing returned to something approaching normal.

Where are they?

At every second he expected to hear the clickety-click. But no noise came.

Then he heard the rumble. His heart leaped as a train blew past in the tunnel, a blur of light and noise and vibration that passed so fast he didn't even have time to be surprised.

His mind raced.

How did things turn to shit so quickly?

He took out a smoke and sucked on it eagerly, trying to find the same calm that he would get while out on his boat crabbing. But it wouldn't come. He kept seeing that suppurating stump, and he jumped at the slightest noise.

I need to get out of here.

He couldn't make himself step back out into the tunnel.

He turned back to the dark passage. Using the lighter he walked in further. It seemed to be a long-disused maintenance duct, the walls little more than rough concrete. The flame on the lighter flickered slightly; a cold draft blowing into his face from ahead.

The lighter wasn't going to last forever. He walked along the passage as fast as he dared. The only noise was the padding of his feet on the dusty ground below.

He came to a corner. There was more light beyond and he was able to put out the lighter. But as soon as he turned the corner he immediately stepped back into the shadows. His heart pounded again, so loud he thought his chest might burst.

Well. I've found the crabs.

He risked a look.

Beyond the corner lay a high vaulted area… another abandoned station. Faded paint-work on the tiling spelled out the station name but it was too worn to read. All he could make out were two letters, a C and a T. High above were brightly coloured tiled arches, rusted chandeliers and grey murky skylights. It had been abandoned for some time, as there was no sign of any rails, and any platform there might have been had crumbled to rubble.

Dim light came from way up above. There might be a possible way out up there, but Porter wasn't thinking about that. He was looking, awe-struck, at the heaving mass of beasts that crammed into the space, some sleeping, others scuttling to and fro on missions to who knows where.

My god. There's hundreds of them.

And it wasn't just the number that amazed him. Many were as big as horses, but others were so big his brain struggled to make sense of it. Out in the middle, surrounded by smaller beasts, sat a grey mound more than twenty-five feet across. It wasn't moving but there was no mistaking that it was a crab. A monster crab.

Porter couldn't quite process the information. The smaller crabs seemed to be delivering food to the larger one; rank after rank of them, like ants feeding a queen. Piles of scat lay everywhere and the stink stung in his nostrils and at the back of his throat.

Over at the far side of the chamber there was a series of four tunnels. These were not man-made, but had been recently dug. Following the ranks of smaller crabs he saw that they were using these tunnels to get in and out of the cavernous space.

He leaned out of the narrow tunnel as far as he dared. He stood on a ledge some ten feet off the floor. On either side of him the walls were smooth with no discernible exits. Away to his right he could just see the darker hole where the old subway tunnel disappeared into blackness. A horde of crabs scuttled and crawled between him and it.

He looked back to the four tunnels opposite. They seemed to stretch away upwards from the cavern floor, and might prove his best hope of escape.

But to get there, I'd have to get across the floor and pass the big one. Ain't no way that's going to happen any time soon.

He hefted the shotgun in his hands. The solidity of it grounded him back in something approaching reality, but he was a long way from feeling calm. He backed away further, back round the corner. The darkness now seemed positively welcoming.

He leaned back against the wall and lit up another smoke.

As far as he could tell his options were limited. There was no way he was going back into the abandoned station. Just thinking about the big crab made him shake and shiver. But going back the way he had come didn't hold much attraction either. He still hadn't forgotten the chorus of *clicking* out in the main subway.

They could still be out there.

Sneaky little fuckers. They'll be waiting for me. But it's the lesser of two evils.

He smoked the cigarette right down to the butt then ground it out beneath his foot. He flicked the lighter into life and started back down the dark passage, back to the main subway tunnel.

He had only got two yards when he heard a distant *rat-a-tat.*

Gunfire?

The noise was joined by a cacophony of *clacking* from back in the disused station. Something had the crabs riled up, and Porter's curiosity got the better of him. He turned back round the corner and looked out over the cavern.

All the smaller crabs headed for the four tunnels opposite, pincers raised, *clacking* in unison like a marching army. He saw now that there were three more of the very large beasts; too big to even get out of the chamber.

They've been growing down here.

The big ones sat still, grey domes that could almost be mistaken for concrete. The other crabs all streamed out of the tunnels. Somewhere in the distance the *rat-a-tat* of gunfire got more insistent.

Someone else is down here. It might be my best chance. I've got to find them.

Porter jumped down into the chamber, holding tight to the shotgun.

31

Shona helped Wilkes haul two team members from the ladder into their side tunnel. The problem was that every member that came up meant one less down below to fight off the attacking crab. The second crab crawled out of the culvert, just behind the first which was already reaching a pincer towards where the team fired round after round. Bullets pinged and ricocheted off the carapace but the crab kept coming.

And Stark is still down there.

She tried to shout above the din.

"Aim for the eyes," she shouted. "Take out the eyes."

The men below didn't hear her. But Wilkes did. He made sure he had firm footing and un-holstered his weapon. The noise level got even worse as he leaned over the shoulder of the men at the mouth of the cave and let off a burst. The crab's left eye *exploded.*

It threw itself forward in fury.

The man next to Stark was taken completely by surprise. A claw nearly six foot long clamped around his waist and clicked. The man fell in two pieces, dead before he had time to scream. The second crab scrambled over the top of the first, reaching over the head of Stark and plucking a climbing man from the ladder. The man tried to turn, raising his weapon, but he wasn't given time to fire. The pincer *squeezed.* Blood spewed from the man's mouth in a fountain. Stark blew the joint of the pincer apart with a close-up burst from less than a yard. The claw fell into the sewer, the man still held in its grasp. His lifeless stare looked back at them until the current took him through the culvert and out of sight.

Despite the best efforts of the team the crabs kept up the attack. Down in the culvert shadows showed against the wall. Pincers, tens of them, waved menacingly in the air.

More crabs are coming.

Wilkes had noticed.

"Get up here," he shouted. "Fast. We've got incoming."

Shona moved aside as the two other men joined Wilkes in setting up covering fire for the other men to come up the ladder. Another wild scream pierced the air above the gunfire.

Stark? Please, don't let it be Stark.

She felt ashamed for the thought, but she couldn't lie to herself any more. She cared deeply about what happened to the Colonel. She looked each man in the face as they came up the ladder.

Stark was last to get to the top. As he pulled himself up into the tunnel his face looked ashen, the strain showing.

"Fall back," he shouted. "Into the tunnel. It's our only hope."

A huge pincer raised up just behind him. Shona screamed. Stark spun and fired in one movement. Bits of shell flew - the bullets at close range doing most damage. But it wasn't going to be near enough. When the firing stopped Shona heard the noise she was coming to fear above all others.

Clickety-click.

She peered between the soldiers and looked into the sewer chamber.

The whole area was a seething mass of scuttling, crawling crabs of sizes ranging from two to twelve feet. They clambered over each other, filling the space, piling high on top of each other, forming a pyramidal mass reaching almost to the level of their feet.

"Fall back," Stark called again. Shona hit the wall as two soldiers forced their way past her to hold a rearguard. Stark grabbed her arm and half-dragged her deeper into the tunnel.

They were pressed close now.

Easy prey.

Beyond the two men in the tunnel mouth the air was full of swaying claw and the loud snap of the pincers coming together. One of the magazines ran empty. He stepped back to reload. He wasn't given time. A huge claw plucked him from the tunnel and he was gone without a sound.

Stark pulled harder at her arm.

"Come on. Time to go."

Indeed, they had almost waited too long. A horde of smaller crabs, still near two feet across themselves, spilled into the tunnel. The man at the entrance went down under a mound, firing a short burst that was quickly silenced.

“Fire in the hold” Wilkes shouted.

This time Shona remembered to turn away and close her eyes. The flash flared in her eyelids, but she barely had time to register it. Her ears filled with a deafening roar. She tasted mud in her mouth, just for a second, before the roof fell on her and everything went black.

32

Porter clambered over large piles of rubble and stood looking over the disused station. Most of the smaller crabs had now left, headed up the tunnels opposite.

But I still have to walk past those big buggers. And I'm not sure I want to do that.

Not just yet.

He walked slowly, carefully, but the large grey domes of the crabs' shells did not move.

He breathed more easily. He wasn't out of the woods, not by a long chalk. But nothing had attacked him for at least five minutes, and that could only be a good thing.

As he got closer to the nearest giant, he noticed a glistening sheen on the ground, one that shifted in the light like oil on water. He moved closer and bent for a closer look. A clump of silver globes lay there, each reflecting his face back at him. They pulsated, almost as if they were breathing.

Eggs.

Small, perfectly formed crabs squirmed inside balls of fluid held together by an oily slime. Porter felt the urge grow to rip and tear at them, to stomp them into mush. He raised a foot.

At the same time a loud blast rang out from above and echoed around the station.

The nearest giant *twitched,* and Porter stopped in mid-kick. He held his breath and backed off, slowly.

The large crab fell quiet again. Porter moved away further, but almost everywhere he wanted to put his feet he found more of the eggs.

Thousands of them. Tens of thousands.

It took him far longer than he wished to navigate the floor of the station. With every step he expected one of the giants to wake and come for him. He clutched tightly at the gun, even though he knew it would be worse than useless if it came down to it. By the time he reached the mouth of the first tunnel he felt like he'd ran for miles, with sweat running in cold runnels down his spine.

He moved quickly into the tunnel and leaned against the wall until his breath slowed and he stopped shaking.

Now that he knew what to look for he studied the floor of the station. As far as he could see, the floor, and even the walls, glistened with the oily slime.

The eggs were everywhere.

A chill ran through him. The numbers he had seen travelling up the tunnels earlier had seemed bad enough. But if these hatched then the whole city could be overrun in no time.

Now he had no more thought of the money; indeed, he had forgotten it completely. His only need now was to get out, anyway he could. After that he would find someone to tell about the eggs, then find the nearest bar.

And I might even change the order in which those two happen.

It was only when his heart slowed and the pounding in his ears dimmed that he realised there was no more noise from above. The shooting had stopped… it had stopped at the same time as the loud blast.

Either the crabs are all dead, or the folks doing the shooting are all dead. Don't matter either way... I have to go up.

He started up the tunnel. Even here some of the slime glistened, but as it got darker away from the abandoned station the tunnel seemed to be drier, almost clean. He walked in silence, expecting at any minute to hear the *clickety-clack.* But there was no sign of any crabs.

Something grew in him, something like hope.

It was soon quashed.

He arrived at a junction. Fresh air came from his left and he chose to follow his nose. He soon wished he hadn't.

The screaming came softly at first, so quiet that he could almost dismiss it as engine noise from trains in the tunnels. But a minute later he could deny it no longer. Somewhere ahead, people were in panic and fear, and he was headed straight for it.

But there was light that way, light and fresher air.

And maybe people with bigger guns. I have to see.

He walked quicker, almost running. He came to a new opening. The debris and still-damp earth told of a recent cave in.

Beyond the hole he looked out into a scene of chaos.

It was a tube station… or rather, it had been. Now, it was a slaughterhouse. Large crabs ran riot through a large crowd of people, snipping and chopping. Limbs flew, blood spurted, and screams echoed loudly in the confined area. Panic reigned everywhere. Not only were the crabs causing carnage, but Porter saw several bodies get trampled underfoot by suited commuters climbing over anything in their way as they searched for escape.

Porter's viewpoint was from a spot at the end of a long curved station platform. A train was lying at a skewed angle off the tracks. Along its length lay the mangled forms of dead passengers amid broken glass and scattered baggage. Right at the far end of the track he saw a large claw, torn from a body, lying next to a uniformed body that had obviously been the driver.

Also up that end, what remained of the commuters tried to funnel their way up a staircase to safety in a rolling maul of thrashing, screaming terror. But the crabs were everywhere, and the blood had thrown them into frenzy.

Claws *snicked.*

Limbs fell from bodies. Blood arced high, splashing on the tiled walls of the tunnel.

Porter sat down, hard, his legs refusing to support him. He dragged himself backward into the tunnel, eyes squeezed shut and hot tears stinging at the corners. He sat there for a long time while claws clacked and the screams slowly faded.

Someone sobbed loudly. It took him some time to realise that he was the one making the noise. He clamped a hand over his mouth. But he still wouldn't… couldn't open his eyes.

All fell silent, but still Porter did not move.

It was only the thought of the eggs that got him going again. If they hatched, then the scene he'd so recently viewed would undoubtedly be played out all over the city.

I have to move. I have to tell someone.

He risked a look into the station. Nothing moved. There were only the scattered torsos and limbs of dismembered bodies. There was no sign of any crabs. But even as he stepped onto the platform and headed for the stairs that would lead him up to fresh air and sky the screams came again.

From above this time.

Crabs were loose in the city.

33

Shona dreamed.

She was ten, and Champion had gone missing. She'd looked everywhere... except one place, the place she wasn't allowed to go. But the pony wasn't in the field, and Shona was getting almost frantic with worry. Her fear for the pony overrode any admonishments she might get. She stepped into her father's study.

The pony wasn't there. The room was cool and quiet, and she suddenly felt guilty at being there. Dad never allowed anyone in here.

She was just about to leave when the noise came again. A wooden chair moved, as if pushed. It fell over with a crash that was loud in the quiet room. One of the stone slabs that made up the floor lifted, and a second later slammed back down into place. Her heartbeat thudded loud in her chest.

'Champion?' she said in a whisper, even though she knew the pony couldn't possibly be under the floor.

She backed away, but not fast enough.

A stone slab flew into the air and something came crawling up out of the hole.

It was big, grey, with milk-white eyes the size of saucers. A leg the thickness of her arm clawed for purchase on the floor and the creature gave a high shrieking whistle of frustration as it tried to push itself out of a hole that seemed to be getting smaller around it.

The floor bucked underneath her, and she almost lost her balance. Stone rasped against stone as slabs were pushed aside.

Pincers waved in the air as more creatures came through. And finally, as she turned and ran, she recognised them for what they were.

They were crabs... giant grabs, grown to the size of Farmer Brown's tractor. She tried to scream, but found her mouth filled with dry soil. Someone called her name, but she couldn't take her eyes off the crabs, scores of the beasts pouring in a flood from father's study.

"Shona!" the shout came again.

She woke with a start, disoriented. Once again she tasted earth in her mouth. She tried to raise a hand, to wipe it away. Her arms seemed pinned to her sides.

"Lie still," the voice said. It was Stark, but there was something she'd never heard in his tone before, something that sounded like panic. She opened her eyes, but closed them again immediately when a bright light, too close, speared into her brain causing almost physical pain. She squirmed.

"For pity's sake," Stark hissed. "Lie still. It's not safe."

She felt someone shift earth by her right side. There was more movement at her left.

"Hurry," she heard Stark whisper. She was lifted bodily, feeling earth fall aside all around her. She spat earth and sucked air. It tasted dry, almost stale, but still preferable to mud. Carefully she opened her eyes. Stark was facing away from her; his headlight no longer aimed at her face. Wilkes stood beside him, the pair of them staring at a mound of fresh earth and stone -- a rock-fall that had completely blocked the tunnel. She looked around. There were only the three of them there. Behind was only a dark tunnel.

"The others?" she whispered.

Wilkes was ashen, unable to speak.

Stark nodded towards the fall.

"In there. The fall got them. We were lucky it didn't get us all."

Shona moved forward, started to claw at the earth. Stark pulled her back.

"Don't you think we haven't tried? It is twenty minutes since the fall." He almost sobbed. "I thought we'd lost everybody. I thought I'd lost *you*."

She continued to try to shovel earth.

"We can't give up," she shouted.

As if in answer, a small avalanche ran down the mound ahead of her.

"There's someone moving," she said. She started shovelling faster. Wilkes pulled her backwards. She turned on him, raising her hand, almost ready to slap his face.

More earth fell.

"Look," she pleaded. "Someone is still alive."

She turned… just in time to see a two-foot white claw emerge from the soil.

"Time to go," Stark said.

"Go where?"

"Anywhere but here," Wilkes replied with a laugh that turned into a sob.

She let herself be led off.

Stark turned and fired a volley into the earth, just as two crabs forced their way out of the dirt. The whole mound heaved and roiled as more beasts pushed their way through. A longer pincer waved in the air. It had a human torso held tightly in its grasp.

Stark fired a final volley then all three of them turned and ran, headlong into the darkness ahead. Behind them the *clickety-clack* of snapping pincers grew to a deafening cacophony.

34

Porter came up out of the subway into a scene from hell.

He had thought that the slow walk up the stairs from below had been the worst he would have to endure. The disembodied limbs, the heads sitting, forlorn, like forgotten footballs, and the slimy rivers of blood and gore… all of that he had suffered, in the hope of something better above ground.

It was not to be.

As soon as he climbed the stairs out of the station he realised where he was. There was no mistaking the shining towers and marble halls of Wall Street.

But it had never looked like this.

The plaza was full of scuttling crabs, each the size of a horse, and some bigger. Terrified men in suits ran like frightened chickens, but the crabs were truly remorseless. The sound of wailing and screaming filled the air, and blood sprayed and gouted over all surfaces. Porter watched one brave man step in front of a large crab, trying to defend a downed man behind him. But his only weapon was a leather briefcase. He managed to bat one pincer aside, but the second took his hand off at the wrist. Still he fought, stepping inside the pincers and clawing at the crab's eyes with his remaining hand, even while his blood sprayed over the shell. He barely slowed the crab at all. It scuttled backwards and sideways in a crude parody of a dance, then, with a final flourish, *snipped* the man in half and stepped over him to its next victim. Porter turned away as a smaller crab leant over the fallen man and started to cut.

But turning his head only brought a new atrocity into view. On the far side of the plaza a bus-load of tourists screamed and thrashed as two huge crabs calmly cut their way into the vehicle, neater than a manual tin-opener and twice as fast. One crab grabbed the bus and *shook* while the second waited at the open end as wailing bodies tumbled and sprawled at its feet and the *snipping* began.

Shots came, echoing among the tall buildings. Four policemen ran into the plaza, guns blazing, trying to distract the large crabs' attention from the bus. They lasted ten seconds before going down under a mound of skittering legs and claws.

Sirens wailed in the distance.

Ain't nobody going to get here in time to save nobody.

More screams came, from further away, outside the plaza.

They're moving out into the city.

God help us all.

So far the crabs had ignored Porter. He stood in the doorway of the subway station, unsure as to his next move. What he wanted to do was to retreat back down the subway, find somewhere to hide, just wait it out and have some smokes.

Let the glory boys sort it out.

He wasn't going to be given that luxury. A higher pitched yell came from the bus. The crab now had the bus held at a near forty-five degree angle and was shaking it, hard. There was only one person still aboard, a young girl, no more than eight years old. She hung by the arms, holding tight to a seat, screaming at the top of her lungs.

Even then Porter considered just turning away.

But I've been doing far too much of that already.

He hefted the shotgun and moved forward at a run. The crab holding the bus didn't notice him until he was less than two yards from it. It dropped the bus, bringing another squeal from the girl. Porter dropped in a roll and tumbled beneath the crab. In the same movement he stuck the shotgun up into the beast's belly, pressing the muzzle hard against the softer area of shell. He pulled the trigger, twice, feeling the shock bang hard against his arm and shoulder. He kept rolling, expecting at any moment to be caught in one of the claws.

Well, this was a great idea.

He got quickly to his feet. He was standing near a large hole cut in the side of the bus. Somewhere the girl still screamed but she was safe, for now. The crab he'd shot staggered around the plaza, scuttling frantically from side to side. It moved at a strange angle, and when it turned he saw why. Only four of its legs were working. It had to drag the whole left-hand side of its body along. The large claw hung at its side, hanging limply, scraping on the ground.

I broke it.

Other crabs started to circle it, including the second large one that had attacked the bus.

Weed out the weak.

The attack was swift and brutal. Although the crab was much larger than most of the attackers it was too badly injured to put up a fight. They were all over it in seconds.

A moan came from next to him.

"Mister, I'm scared."

The small girl stood there. Tears had streaked her cheeks, and her eyes were red from crying.

"Me too," Porter said. "Let's get out of here. Okay?"

She nodded and lifted up her arms. It took him seconds to realise she wanted to be carried.

He looked around. The crabs were all otherwise occupied. Indeed, they seemed to be thinning out, moving further afield in the city looking for fresh meat.

The girl looked down and saw the gore at their feet. She squeezed her eyes tightly shut. Tears were close again. He lifted the girl in his left arm. She clung tightly to his neck… too tightly, but strangely the small display of humanity affected him.

He had tears in his own eyes as they moved away from the ruined bus.

35

Stark led them through a warren of dark tunnels, running at almost full pelt until Shona could hardly breathe.

"Stop," she whispered. "I have to stop."

She bent over, sucking air in whooping gulps. Her head buzzed. At some point she'd bruised her left side from the shoulder all the way down to her hip. It throbbed hotly in time with her heartbeat.

Behind them, distant but closing, she heard the sound she was coming to dread.

Clickety-clack.

"We need to keep moving," Stark said softly, putting a hand on her shoulder.

"But where?" she managed. "Do you have any idea where we are?"

Wilkes held up a GPS system, its small green screen casting a glow on his face.

"It's only working intermittently," he said. "But as far as I can tell we're somewhere under Broadway."

"Give it my regards," Shona said, but trying to laugh brought on a fit of coughing. The sounds echoed around them. A second later the clacking behind them got louder and more insistent.

Shona managed to straighten up. Stark was about to speak but she stopped him with a quick kiss on his cheek.

"I know… time to go. Just do me a favour. Find us a way out of here, quickly. I'm not sure how much further I can run."

Wilkes came to her rescue.

"Maybe we won't have to. Over here sir."

He motioned over to their left. While Stark had his back turned he dropped her a wink.

"I've never known a team member to get away with kissing the boss before," he said, smiling.

Stark turned back.

"Buy me a beer when we get out and I might let you," he said. He reached out a hand and Shona took it. He led her to a narrow side tunnel.

""'Looks like our boy here was right," Stark said. "There's an access hatch in here, and a ladder."

"Where does it go?"

"Up," Wilkes said. "Shall I take point sir?"

Stark nodded and Wilkes went into the tunnel. His voice came back, echoing around them.

"All clear."

The *clacking* had grown much louder.

"After you," Stark said. He leaned over and kissed her on the lips. "That's a promise of more later. And you won't even have to buy me a beer."

Shona followed Wilkes. The Lieutenant had a hatchway open and his head stuck through looking upwards. Beyond him she saw a steel stepladder.

"There's daylight up there," he said. "About a hundred feet or so. Can you handle that?"

Shona nodded.

"I'll be right behind you."

But by the time she put her first hand on the ladder he was already six feet above her and accelerating away. She knew she was going to be in trouble as soon as she had gone up one step. Pain flared in her ribs -- a white heat that threatened to throw her into unconsciousness.

Something's bust in there.

Stark arrived beneath her.

"Are you okay?"

"I will be," she said. But I won't be winning any speed trials."

She looked down. Stark's worried eyes looked back at her.

"Just go at your own pace," he said. He turned and tried to close the hatch. He gave it a tug… and it fell to the floor with a loud clang. As the echo faded, loud clacking came from what sounded like just outside.

"Go," Stark shouted. "I'll be right behind you."

She turned back to the ladder. Even as she pulled herself up another rung Stark started shooting. The shaft was filled with light and noise. Wilkes looked down.

"Keep going," Shona shouted. "We need to get some height."

When she was eight feet up she looked down. Stark pumped round after round towards the open hatchway. Several claws tried to reach him. But it looked like the beasts themselves were too large to get through… for now.

"Stark. Get your arse up here," she shouted.

He turned and saluted sarcastically.

"Yes ma'am."

She started to climb. She felt vibrations on the ladder as Stark followed. Below him metal screeched and tore.

They're cutting through.

High above her Wilkes was nearing the top; so far above that she could barely see him in the dim light.

Stark had climbed up and reached her feet in seconds.

"How are you doing?" he shouted.

The pain was almost unbearable.

But the alternative is much worse.

"I'll live," she said, and went back to climbing.

The noises from below grew louder and once more the insistent *clacking* returned.

Stark started firing, but Shona could not look back. Her whole being was concentrated on the next step, and the next after that.

Inch by slow inch, she climbed.

36

Porter, the child still clinging tightly to him, inched along, back to the wall. In all the buildings around the plaza, people pressed their faces to the windows, gawkers at the scene of the biggest wreck in history. Several had cups of coffee and sandwiches in their hand.

I'm surprised they're not giving out fucking popcorn.

Porter waved the shotgun towards them. Some retreated, fast. One fat bastard in a suit gave Porter the finger.

If I didn't have this little girl here, that fucker would be dead already.

He made a play of pulling the trigger and the fat man smiled back at him, as if this was some kind of fucking game.

Things didn't get any better. With his next step his foot met something soft that *squished* underfoot, like a wet cowpat. He didn't want to look down, but his foot had got caught. His left heel was sunk into the spilled guts of a young woman. Her dead eyes stared accusingly at him as he disentangled himself from the warm offal. He'd been so intent on rescuing the girl that he hadn't quite realised the scale of the catastrophe that had hit the plaza. Bodies lay strewn everywhere, blood, gore and guts steaming slightly. Black flies had descended, as if from nowhere. Over by the subway a stray dog picked up a loose foot and slunk off with it.

Two small crabs hunched over a police car, picking flesh from a body that hung half-out of a broken windshield. From the streets beyond came the sounds of further mayhem; screams rent the air, horns blazed and shots echoed among the buildings. And above that, the sound he believed he'd be hearing in his sleep for evermore, the loud clacking of crab claws.

He had another longing look at the subway entrance.

Might be safest down there.

Then he remembered the walk along the platform; the press of the dead, tightly packed, limbs strewn asunder, strips of flesh ripped off, exposing gore and bone beneath. He couldn't subject the little girl to that. It had nearly finished him, never mind a child.

He kept moving, sidling along the side of the building. The noise got louder. The girl whimpered and stuck her face in his neck. He felt her hot tears, and thought once more of Sarah.

This is doing no good at all. One of then fuckers could be along at any moment.

He stepped round the corner.

A pitched battle raged along Broadway. A line of army vehicles had just completed blockading the street. The noise reached a deafening din as they started firing bullets, grenades and missiles into the massed ranks of crabs. Porter ducked involuntarily as a chopper screamed overhead and laid down fire, blasting shell and claw into tiny fragments. Suddenly the air smelled of roasting crab. Much to his disgust Porter found himself salivating.

He could see no way to reach the army line… the space between here and there was filled with a heaving mass of crabs. And although the army was doing terrible damage, still the beasts kept moving forward. Some of them had almost reached the defensive line. The rate of fire from the glory boys went up a notch. Crabs seemed to *dance,* pincers raised. And still they came forward.

They *surged.*

The defences failed almost immediately.

But the army boys had been prepared for that. They fell back fast, leaving their vehicles behind. The crabs started to climb and crawl over the trucks and jeeps. They paid no attention to the chopper that came back for another pass.

It strafed the crabs… and the vehicles. The whole width of the street went up with a *whump.*

Porter had to retreat fast from the sudden blast of heat. Even so he felt the skin of his face tighten and smelled burnt hair as his eyebrows singed. The girl whimpered again but didn't raise her head.

Suddenly everything went quiet.

Shit. I've gone deaf.

He looked round, just as the noise of the city started to fill in around him. Fires crackled all along the street, metal pinged in the heat. In the distance he heard a solitary *clickety-clack*, but there was no movement from any of the crabs from the attack… all that was left was burnt and burning shell.

On the far side of the barricade troops moved forward, cautiously at first and then with more confidence as the crabs stayed down.

Porter walked towards them… only to find himself facing down the barrels of six automatic rifles.

"Put the gun down sir," someone shouted.

I'd forgotten I even had it!

He bent and laid the gun at his feet. A soldier came over, still with his weapon trained on Porter, and kicked the shotgun away. It was only then that the soldiers relaxed.

"The girl, is she injured?" one of them asked.

"I don't think so. But she's in shock," Porter replied.

"I know how she feels," the soldier muttered. "There's a field hospital being set up a hundred yards down the road. Can you make it that far?"

Porter nodded. That was enough for the soldiers. They immediately forgot about him.

Clickety-clack.

The noise came from back in the plaza at the subway station. Half of the troops left at a run. More jeeps and trucks were being brought up along Broadway. Curious soldiers stared out at Porter as he carried the girl along the street he no longer recognised.

Dead lay everywhere… dead, and pieces of the dead.

The girl started to squirm and lifted her head from his neck. Gently he pushed it back in place.

"Not long now sweetheart. Just close your eyes for a bit longer."

He found the medical unit seconds later. They were in the process of setting up a field hospital in the middle of the street. Several wounded men were already being worked on frantically by surgeons wearing bloody tunics. More screams rose, and the girl stiffened in his arms. He squeezed her gently.

"It's okay darling. You're safe now."

A nurse finally took notice of him. She had to coax the girl to let go of Porter's neck, but when the child was taken away, she immediately grabbed the nurse in the same way. She looked back at Porter as they left but there was no recognition in her eyes.

She's got a hard road back from this.

But at least she was alive. A great many folk hadn't made it. Porter lit a cigarette and was almost immediately hustled out of the med-tent by a disapproving nurse. As he stood in the middle of Broadway the sheer scale of the disaster started to dawn on him. One of the busiest streets, in one of the world's biggest cities, had been turned into a war zone in minutes… by a bunch of crabs.

It was then that he remembered the disused station and the nest below. He ground out the cigarette and went back into the med-tent in search of an officer.

37

Shona thought the climb would never end. The pain was excruciating… a white flare of heat that felt like it had burned her bones. She concentrated on putting one foot above the other and climbing, one step at a time.

She stopped, just once, heart pounding and breath coming hot and fast.

Stark shouted from below.

"Is there a problem?"

It was seconds before she could reply.

"Just need a rest," she whispered. "Give me a minute."

She looked down, and gasped. The shaft below Stark was a rolling mass of small crabs, none more than a foot across clambering over each other in a frantic attempt to reach Stark's feet. They were no more than eighteen inches away from achieving it. The *clicking* of their pincers only registered as her breathing slowed and her heartbeat returned to something approaching normal.

"I'd suggest thirty seconds might be better," Stark said calmly. He turned, looked down and sent a volley of shots into the beasts. That slowed them down… but not for long.

"I see what you mean," she said.

She went back to the climb, taking it as fast as she was able. She was dimly aware of Stark shooting again, twice more, but she couldn't waste the effort to take any heed. Her life shrunk to the six inches in front of her eyes… that, and the next rung to be tackled. Her brain kept itself busy calculating how many rungs she'd travelled, how long each took, and how long it might take to get to the top. There were several variables she had to estimate, but that just made it a more difficult, more absorbing task for her to tackle… anything to keep her mind off the pain.

She was surprised when her head hit something… Lieutenant Wilkes' foot.

"Fifth floor, Haberdashery and Lingerie," Wilkes said, deadpan.

She laughed, then groaned as a new pain hit.

Wilkes suddenly looked worried.

"You don't look so hot ma'am," he said.

"I bet you say that to all the girls."

Wilkes bent down and lifted her onto a small platform below a large grate. Stark pulled himself up to join them.

"We're in trouble sir," Wilkes said.

Stark laughed grimly.

"I'd spotted that."

"No. *More* trouble."

Wilkes reached up and banged on the grate with his gun. It seemed to be built of cast iron. It clanged but didn't move.

"It's solid. I can't move it."

Stark reached up and shook it. Some small pieces of rust fell in their hair but nothing else wanted to move.

"Cover us," Stark said to Wilkes. He twiddled with his ear-piece.

"This is Colonel Stark. Can anyone hear me?"

Shona heard a crackle and a fragmented voice trying to come through. Wilkes fired a long burst down in the shaft at the same time, drowning out any other response.

"Sorry sir," he said as he turned back. "Best make it quick. They're getting close."

Stark tried again. This time the reply came through clearer.

"We've got you sir. ETA four minutes."

Wilkes turned at that. He looked pale.

"I doubt we have that much time sir."

"We'll have to make time."

Stark joined Wilkes standing over the shaft. Both men fired long volleys down into the crabs, emptying their magazines and slapping new ones into place with barely a pause. The air in the chamber got hot and acrid. Shona finally remembered she had a weapon of her own. She stood over the shaft and stared down.

Her father's worst nightmare had been made flesh. The whole shaft seethed with crustaceans, all between nine inches and a foot across, pincers snapping frantically. In their frenzy they chopped pieces out of the crabs around them, but still they came, clambering over the top of their dead. They were little more than two feet below the lip, and coming fast.

Shona fired her weapon, the recoil slamming fresh pain up and down her ribcage.

All too soon she ran out of ammo.

"Do you have a clip for me?"

Stark didn't pause in his firing.

"I never thought we'd need one," he shouted.

"What do you think now," she said, sarcastically, as the first crab climbed over the lip. She stomped on it, hard, and kicked it back into the throng where it was chopped and diced in seconds.

Stark was now too busy to reply.

"I'm on my last clip," Wilkes shouted.

"Me too," Start replied.

All three of them now had to stomp and tramp in a manic dance, *squishing* crabs underfoot, the crack of shell breaking loud even amid the gunfire.

Snick!

Warm blood ran from a cut just above Shona's ankle.

The first of many.

The men kept firing.

The noise was deafening. Shona's eyes hurt from the flash and flicker from the muzzles. She looked away, up to the grate… just as a shadow passed above.

"Down here," she called. "We're down here!"

More shadows moved above. The grate started to slide to one side.

"Guys. Time to go."

An arm reached down from above.

She grabbed it and was lifted, one armed, up through to daylight. New pain threatened to engulf her completely, but the sound of a scream from below rooted her back in reality.

Stark!

She turned just in time to see Wilkes pull himself out of the grate opening. Five crabs nipped and cut at his legs, blood seeping through his trousers.

Another shout of pain came from below. The soldier beside Wilkes leaned over the grate and sent a long burst of bullets down into the shaft. Two others jumped down into the hole. Seconds later they bundled a prone figure out. Wilkes helped and they lay the Colonel on the ground.

Shona's heart leaped.

Stark!

She bent over him. His lower torso was a mass of small cuts, but as she bent over him he opened his eyes and smiled.

"See. I told you I'd show you a good time."

38

At first Porter couldn't find anyone to listen to him.

"Listen sir," the first officer he approached said. "You can see we've got a situation here. Please, just let us do our job."

The second was even more dismissive.

"Sit down and shut up, or I'll shoot you."

Porter cut that one some slack. The man was covered in blood and smelled of crabmeat.

He's been in the front line. And he's seen what the fuckers can do.

Porter was just about ready to go outside for another smoke when a truck pulled up and three more injured were unloaded. He heard one of them being referred to as Colonel.

I haven't spoken to anyone higher than Major yet. One last try. If this is a bust, I'm outta here.

The Colonel was laid on a gurney and nurses started to work on his wounds. They all looked nasty, but none seemed life threatening. Porter took his chance and stepped forward.

"Colonel?"

A nurse started to hustle him away.

"I found a nest," Porter shouted. "With thousands of eggs."

The tent went deathly quiet. The nurse started to hustle Porter away once more, but the officer sat up.

"Let him through nurse."

Closer up Porter saw the same look in this man's eyes he'd seen earlier.

This one's also been up close and personal with the fuckers.

A woman walked over to stand at the Colonel's side. She winced as she walked, and her eyes had the same look as the others.

"Tell me," she said.

Porter looked at the Colonel.

"You heard what Ms Menzies said," the officer replied. "She's the one with the answers."

So he told his story

He missed out the part about the young security guard at the zoo, but more or less got everything else told. They listened in silence until he described the scene in the disused subway. Just talking about it brought the scene rushing back.

As he gets closer to the nearest giant, he notices a glistening sheen on the ground, one that shifts in the light like oil on water. He moves closer and bends for a closer look. A clump of silver globes lies there, each reflecting his face back at him. They pulsate, almost as if they are breathing.

Eggs.

Small, perfectly formed crabs squirm inside balls of fluid held together by an oily slime.

"How many?" the Colonel asked.

Porter remembered the sheer scale, the enormity, of the nest area.

"Thousands. Tens of thousands. Maybe more."

"It's not possible," someone whispered.

The Menzies woman looked solemn.

"I'm afraid it's all too possible. We knew they were looking for something. They were looking for a nesting ground."

"And they found it," Porter said.

"So what do we do now?" the third officer who'd been brought in said.

"We have to go back in," the Menzies woman replied. "Go in, and clear them out."

The Colonel laughed bitterly.

"In case you hadn't noticed, we didn't do too well the last time we went down there."

"But we have to," the woman said. "If these things hatch then what's happened today will seem like a picnic. The whole of Manhattan will be in their feeding territory."

The Colonel sat up as the nurses finished applying the field dressings to his wounds.

"So what's the plan?"

The woman seemed stumped.

Porter's mouth worked before his brain.

"Only one way to clean out a crab burrow. Burn them out. I've found that gasoline usually works."

Once again the place went quiet. The army boys all stared at him, mouths open.

Mama always told me that my mouth would get me into trouble one of these days.

The Menzies woman spoke first.

"That might work."

The Colonel nodded.

"And I think we can come up with something better than gasoline. But first we need to find the place."

He turned back to Porter.

"Do you remember the name of the station?"

Porter shook his head.

"But I can tell you how to get there."

"Too risky. We might take a wrong turn. No. You'll have to show us."

The Colonel took a new set of trousers from an orderly.

"Wilkes?"

The other officer looked up.

"I need ten men with Napalm B flame units. And I need them yesterday."

"Yes sir."

Wilkes saluted and left the tent.

The Colonel stood and clapped Porter on the arm.

"Well, it looks like you just got conscripted."

39

Half an hour later Shona stood at the entrance to the Wall Street Subway station, looking down into the dark. Three soldiers had already gone down. The crabber, Porter, was at her side. He looked even less enthusiastic than she felt.

"You're sure we have to do this?" he asked.

Shona nodded.

"But you don't have to," she replied. "You're not military. They can't force you."

Porter ground out a cigarette.

"I'm going," he said. "I owe it to some people."

Her ribs still hurt, but some painkillers had taken the edge off it. If truth be told, what she was really feeling was excitement. No nest of the mutant crabs had ever been found. This was an opportunity of a lifetime. She'd packed some kit in a backpack.

I just hope I get a chance to use it.

Just to her right Stark and Wilkes were deep in discussion with a very pale-looking subway official. The man was getting increasingly animated and, more than that, terrified. Shona wondered what Stark was asking of the man.

No less than he'd ask of himself.

The city around them had fallen eerily silent. It had been five minutes since the last sound of distant gunfire. Now it was like a quiet Sunday morning here in Wall Street Plaza.

Apart from the dead folks. And the crabs.

There was enough crab parts scattered around to keep a team of researchers in work for months. She realised that, if she survived the trip down to the nest, that she'd probably be busy for the rest of her life.

I'll be just like Dad.

Stark and Wilkes arrived at her side. Both men moved almost as stiffly as she did, but both looked resolute. They had heavy flame-thrower units strapped on their backs.

"Are you sure that will do enough damage?" she asked.

"It's Napalm B," Stark said. He looked grim. "I've seen it used before. Trust me… it does enough damage."

Seven more men arrived at the station entrance. They too wore flame units and carried automatic weapons.

Stark spoke to Porter.

"Were there any beasts in this station?" he said, nodding to the stairs.

"Only dead ones," Porter replied. "And a lot of dead folks. It ain't pretty."

Stark turned to Shona.

"Last chance. You don't have to come along."

Shona didn't reply. She started down the steps and Porter followed close behind.

The first body was only two steps down; a suited businessman reaching, arm outstretched, for freedom. His lower torso was five steps below the rest of him, his intestines forming a gory bridge between.

That was only the first of many gruesome sights. Shona tried to keep her eyes fixed on the back of the soldier in front of her, but the dead seemed to call out for recognition, for some indications that their pain had some meaning. She found she could not avert her eyes, even when the victims were babes tumbled from parent's arms, or the old and infirm, trampled to death by the fleeing mob. She had tears in her eyes now, tears which hid *some* of the carnage.

But not enough. Tears will never be enough.

Shona hadn't realised it, but they had walked the whole length of the station platform.

Porter pointed at a new-made hole in the wall nearby.

"I came through there."

Shona wasn't paying attention. She stared, wide eyed, at a baby, no more than six months old, sliced neatly in two pieces. She wondered whether she'd ever again see anything quite so sad. She was so lost in her grief that she didn't notice that the soldiers in front of her had stopped. She almost walked into the back of the nearest one.

Stark moved past her.

"What's the problem soldier?" he asked.

"We've got movement ahead sir… in the main tunnel."

Even as the soldier spoke the noise she'd been dreading came.

Clickety-clack.

A shadow loomed on the wall of the tunnel. The crab that came though was nearly nine feet across. Its pincers grazed the roof of the tunnel.

"Burn it," Stark shouted.

The front three soldiers all fired up their flame-throwers at the same time. Fire rolled over the shell and *stuck.*

"Cease fire!" Stark shouted. "Save it for later."

The soldiers took their fingers off the triggers. The flame kept burning, a bright yellow that left its impression behind Shona's eyes. The crab thrashed, pincers knocking tiles off the subway wall. The team stepped back as it threatened to climb off the track, but the flames had it in a tight hold. It slumped to one side. One of the pincers slapped, one last time, on the edge of the platform, then it was still.

The flames burned for a long time while the team looked on.

The crab stayed down.

Stark looked over at Shona.

"Effective enough for you?"

40

Porter led the team through the hole into the tunnels. The closer he got to the nest, the less he wanted to be there. But every time he thought of running, he saw the girl in his mind, and Sarah looking accusingly back from her young face. That, and the fact that having a well armed team around him, ensured that he kept going, no matter how much his legs told him it was a bad idea.

The tunnels were quiet as they descended. There wasn't even the distant hum of tube trains to disturb the silence.

They'll have the whole system shut down by now. The city will be at a standstill.

The enormity of the situation hit him. The fate of the city hung on him leading this team to the right place.

I'm finally important.

And I don't like the feeling.

Scant weeks ago he'd been out in his cabin on the Bay, wishing for a way out. Now he'd give anything to be back there, just drifting offshore with a hip flask and a pack of smokes, and Sarah waiting when he got back. That now seemed a *long* way away. And getting further away by the minute as they kept descending.

When they were getting close, Porter stopped and approached Stark.

"It's just round the next corner," he said.

Stark nodded, and led the team forward.

Porter stood alone for several seconds, looking back up the tunnel, then turned and went to join the others.

41

Shona couldn't quite believe what she was looking at.

She looked over the high vaulted area that bounded the abandoned subway station. Dim light came from way up above. Out in the middle, surrounded by glistening slime, sat four grey mounds, each more than twenty-five feet across. None of them moved but there was no mistaking that they were crabs.

That's impossible.

Piles of scat lay everywhere and the stink stung in her nostrils and at the back of her throat. Away to her left she could just see the darker hole where the old subway tunnel disappeared into blackness. A score of smaller crabs scuttled and crawled around the larger beasts, each of them the size of a horse.

"Now what?" she whispered to Stark.

But the Colonel already had a plan, and he wasted no time in getting it into action.

"We wait," he said. "Lieutenant, do we have a signal?"

Wilkes studied the GPS.

"Yes sir. It seems this station is still on the grid. The plan will work. Sending co-ordinates now."

"Plan?" Shona asked.

Stark gave her a thin smile.

"Some of the tracks around here are still live. We've got a train getting packed with napalm up top and it'll be sent down any minute now." He paused and looked over the nest. "We're going to send this lot to hell."

Shona noticed a glistening at her feet. She stooped to investigate a patch of the eggs.

"We may not have much time."

The young crabs were already starting to cut their way out of their slimy prisons.

Soon there'll be thousands of them. And they'll all be looking for food.

"They're hatching," she said.

Out across the station the slimy coating started to seethe and boil as countless crabs were born.

"How long?" Stark said to Wilkes.

"ETA five minutes."

Young crabs, ranked already like an advancing army, started to march across the floor of the station, heading for the tunnels.

"We've got to stop them," Shona shouted. "Any one of them could grow into a monster."

"The train will be here…"

"We can't afford to wait."

"And what if one of those giants wakes up?"

"We need to take the risk. We can't let *any* escape into the city."

"You heard what the lady said," Wilkes shouted. "Light them up."

Stark held up three fingers, then two, then one.

Then all hell broke loose.

The first burst of napalm washed over the advancing crabs and set a large patch of them aflame. The air filled with the *crack* and *sizzle* of burning shell and soft meat. The horse-sized crabs at the far end of the station turned as one, and mounted a charge. At the same time the new-borns surged sideways, like a wave breaking on a shore, heading en-masse for the open tunnels to the side of the team.

"Fan out," Stark called. "Don't let any escape."

The team spread to cover the tunnels. A flood of napalm washed over the station floor. The larger crabs reached the edge of it and barely slowed. They threw themselves into the flames. Most perished as the inferno took them. Two made it through, shell on fire, pincers smoking, coming at the defenders as if rising straight from hell. More napalm sprayed the first and it tumbled in a jumble of legs and claws.

The second kept coming, barrelling into two men sending them falling to the ground.

Shona felt Stark pull her backwards, hard, into the tunnel.

"Get down," Stark shouted. But he was too late. The backpack of one of the fallen went up with a *whump.* Hot air blew like a hurricane through the tunnels and flame rolled across the roof overhead. She felt skin tighten at her cheeks. The air choked her, too hot to breathe. She held her breath as the heat threatened to bake them alive. For long seconds her ears filled with a roaring bellow as the flame ate the air.

Then, as quickly as it had come, it was gone. She let out her breath and sucked dry, hot air until her heart rate slowed to something approaching normal.

Stark pulled her to her feet.

There were six of them left alive. Wilkes and Porter were on the other side of the tunnel and two soldiers were just getting to their feet. Of the others there was no sign.

A lake of fire lay just in front of the cave. Things lay there… so far burned that Shona could not tell whether they had once been crab… or human.

Beyond the fire the four huge domes started to move. A white pincer the size of a truck waved in the air.

The giants had woken up.

42

Once more Porter's every nerve wanted to run. But the army men stood firm, and so did the Menzies woman. Pride, if nothing else, kept him in place.

The huge crabs in the background were coming awake slowly, sluggishly.

A movement in the far-left tunnel caught his eye. A subway train with its lights full on rumbled into the station. It ground to a halt in a cloud of dust. Metal screeched and the sound echoed loudly around them.

Stark was immediately on the move, sidling round the edge of the napalm lake.

"Are you sure this is a good idea?" Porter asked, but the soldiers, and the woman, had already moved out.

Porter followed, cautiously at first, then faster as the soldiers picked up the speed.

The small group of six managed to skirt the fires. But they had only travelled a third of the way towards the train when the first of the giants stood full up on its legs. When it raised up further and showed them its belly the claws towered nearly twenty yards above them.

We're not going to make it.

Wilkes moved to the back of the line, putting himself between the crab and the others.

"Lead them out Colonel. I'll hold here as long as I can."

He sent out a long wet flame that hung in the air before falling to burn at the base of the crab.

Stark had to forcibly drag the Menzies woman away. They hurried on. Porter looked back, just once. Wilkes was still retreating towards them, keeping the crab at bay with a wall of flame. Napalm ran up the whole right hand side of the beast. It flailed in a frenzied dance, as if trying to catch the fire. The Lieutenant kept himself just out of its reach, buying the fleeing group enough time to reach the train.

A second crab had other ideas. It scuttled across the station, covering ground fast. Stark and the other soldiers created a solid wall of plasma that poured down over it. A milky white eye, near two feet across, *popped*, the viscous fluid hissing as it fell to the ground. Napalm fell in a sheet across the whole length of the beast's back. The shell cracked, like a sudden rifle shot. Stark followed up the napalm with a close up blast from his automatic weapon while the other two men kept pouring flame.

Wilkes joined them. His face was black, his eyebrows singed completely off. Porter risked a look in the direction from which the man had come. Another fire blazed there, a slowly collapsing dome being all that remained of the beast.

"One down sir," Wilkes said.

He joined the others in washing the attacking crab in fire.

After what seemed like minutes the beast finally fell.

By then the third, and fourth crabs had risen up and were nearly on them.

"Run," Stark shouted. "Head for the train."

Porter started to move. His feet sucked at the ground. He looked down to see that they were wading through a thick carpet of more eggs, all near hatching.

They had no time to stop and investigate. Stark and Wilkes took point with Porter and Menzies sandwiched between them and the two other soldiers.

Porter was so intent on watching ahead of them that the first sign they were in trouble was a scream from behind them. He turned to see a soldier held tight in the claw of an eight-foot crab that was still pulling itself out of a pile of rubble.

Snick.

He saw Sarah again as the man fell in two pieces.

The fallen soldier's partner hosed the crab, screaming in rage. He was so far gone in his revenge that he didn't see the third of the giant beasts loom over him.

"Stark!" Porter cried. "We've got incoming."

Stark turned, just as the raging soldier got scooped high in the air. He poured napalm all over the attacking crab, even as the massive pincer squeezed and the man got squished to a lump of raw meat in less than a second. Fresh napalm squirted from the punctured tank, catching fire and spraying in a high arc over the station.

"Run. Get to the train," Stark shouted. "It's our only hope."

Napalm burned all over the crab. It slumped and fell forward into the flame, but behind it Porter saw the fourth loom, pincers raised high.

He turned and ran as flame fell around them.

43

Shona was first to reach the train. A startled driver stared out, wide eyed, unable to take his eyes from the attacking crabs. She ran up towards him… and realised that, without the platform, the open door was nearly four feet high. She tried to pull herself up. The pain in her ribs flared, like a renewed blast of hot flame. She had to stand back, breathing hard, a cold sweat on her brow. She had just mustered enough will to try again when she got boosted at the waist and almost thrown into the train. Porter let go of her and climbed in beside her.

"Sorry," he smiled. "You were in my way."

Outside Stark and Wilkes laid down a covering wall of flame from a position next to the door.

The driver, all blood drained from his face, came out of his cab to join them.

He took one look at the huge crab that loomed beyond the flames and took off, heading away through the train.

There's a way out.

"Stark!" she shouted. "We can get out through the back of the train."

Stark turned and gave her a quick okay.

He kept flaming the area in front of the crab while Wilkes climbed up beside Shona. Her ribs flared again as she helped him up. She tasted blood in her mouth.

Something's definitely bust in there.

She hoped she had time to worry about it later.

Now it was Wilkes' turn to lay down cover. Seconds later all four of them were in the doorway.

"Check the goods," Stark said. Wilkes moved quickly to inspect the barrels that lined the carriage.

"Enough napalm to blow this whole site," he replied.

Stark sent a long sheet of flame towards the crab.

"Okay. Move. We'll light it up from the far end"

All four of them set off down the carriage. Shona saw immediately that it wasn't going to work. The huge crab outside scuttled sideways, and used the lull in firing to close in on the train. Stark went back to the door and sent another flame in its direction. The napalm came up short, but at least the crab had stopped its approach.

Stark looked grim again.

"Get moving then Lieutenant. Get Ms. Menzies and Porter out of here. I'll stay here and make sure it blows."

"No!" Shona shouted. "That's suicide."

Stark looked calm as he stared back at her.

"It's my job Shona. It's what I do."

She went to his side and put a hand on his arm.

"There must be another way," she said.

"There is," he said. "I can order Wilkes to stay. And he would."

"Wanna bet on that sir?" Wilkes said with a smile.

Stark turned back to Shona.

"But we both know I can't do that. Someone has to stay and make sure the job gets done. Today that someone is me."

He looked over at Wilkes and nodded.

Wilkes grabbed Shona by the arm and started to pull her away down the train.

44

Porter was itching to get going. The huge crab outside inched ever closer. He could barely take his eyes off it.

Stark stood at the train door, sending gouts of flame towards the beast.

Porter was smart enough to realise that the backpacks weren't inexhaustible. At some point they were going to run out.

And that's when the real fun will start.

Wilkes started to pull the woman down the train.

Finally. Let's get the fuck out of here.

But she changed everything. Just two short words.

"Help me," she said, her eyes pleading, looking straight at him.

Porter looked at her, and once more saw Sarah. The big crab held her… *the big crab that had turned up looking for the smaller one.* He looked out at the huge crab, then down at the ground outside the train where new-borns were cutting their way out of the slime.

He walked back up the train, past a startled Wilkes, and addressed Stark.

"You can be a glory boy another day. I've got an idea."

Before Stark could stop him he jumped out of he train and started shovelling a slippery mess of slime, eggs and newly hatched crabs up into the train.

Stark fired another warming blast then shouted at him.

"What the hell do you think you're doing?"

Porter smiled.

"Saving your ass. Watch."

He lifted some eggs and crushed, feeling shell crack between his fingers.

The giant crab went into frenzy, huge pincers banging on the ground, hard enough to make the train rattle on its track.

"They protect their young. That's *their* job. That's what *they* do.

The Menzies woman smiled.

"Of course. I should have seen it earlier.

She jumped down beside Porter and helped him haul pile after pile of the eggs onto the floor of the train.

Porter climbed back into the carriage and helped the woman up.

"Okay glory boy. Your turn. How do we trigger the napalm at a distance?

Stark smiled.

"That's the fun bit. Wilkes… your pack. Time to leave a trail."

Wilkes took off his pack and punctured the tank with a knife. Napalm started to spill on the floor. Young crabs *squirmed* in the noxious fluid, and outside the giant slapped on the ground and started to advance, coming fast.

"Okay. Time to see if this plan of yours will work. On three…run.

45

They ran along the length of the train, banging through doors and slapping hard against seats and poles all the way. Wilkes dragged his backpack behind them, leaving a long slick all the way up the train.

Shona's ribs felt like they were on fire.

But it's working.

The huge crab's attention was all on the eggs they had left in the napalm in the end carriage.

Wilkes reached the end of the train first. He helped Shona down.

"Get into the tunnel," he shouted. "As far in as you can. It's going to be a hell of a bang."

Porter and Shona headed for the tunnel. Shona was relieved to see there was no slime or eggs in this area. The only crab in sight was the remaining giant, hunched over the tube train as if it was a tasty morsel.

They reached the tunnel mouth and turned back.

She was just in time to see Stark send a burst of napalm into the train.

Wilkes and Stark turned and ran.

Flame shot all along the trail they had left, running the full length of the train in a heartbeat.

The world went away in a yellow flash.

46

Porter woke in a world of pain. It felt worse than his worst hangover.

No mean feat.

But I'm alive.

The world filled in around him slowly.

He lay on a gurney, in a medical tent that might well be the same one he'd been in earlier. All around him people moved, a buzz of activity. But no matter how hard he listened, there was no gunfire. And no *clacking.*

He sat up. He immediately wished he hadn't as the world span, but it righted itself soon enough.

"He's awake," someone said.

He looked towards the voice.

The young girl he'd saved earlier took a running jump into his arms and kissed him on the cheek.

Suddenly he was smiling.

"Nice plan," a voice said beside him.

The Menzies woman was at the next bed, standing over Stark who was once more being bandaged up. A cut ran down his cheek, and one arm showed the long streak of a blistered burn, but he too smiled as he looked over.

"We made it," Stark said. "Thanks to you."

"The crabs?"

"Cleanup team hasn't found any. They've been all through the tunnels and there's no sign. The teams up in the city arte saying the same thing. I think we got them all."

"And Wilkes?"

"Off looking for some beer."

"Now that *is* a good idea."

Stark reached out a hand. Porter leaned over and shook it.

"We owe you one Mr Porter. Is there anything your government can do for you?"

Porter didn't even have to think about it.

"Well…the crabs destroyed my cabin, I could do with getting it rebuilt. I kinda liked that old place."

THE END

Check out other great

Sea Monster Novels!

Robert J. Stava

NEPTUNES RECKONING

At the easternmost end of Long Island lies a seaside town known as Montauk. Ground Zero on the Eastern seaboard for all manner of conspiracy theories involving it's hidden Cold War military base, rumors of time-travel experiments and alien visitors... For renowned Naval historian William Vanek it's the where his grandfather's ship went down on a Top Secret mission during WWII code-named "Neptune's Reckoning". Together with Marine Biologist Daniel Cheung and disgraced French underwater explorer Arnaud Navarre, he's about to discover the truth behind the urban legends: a nightmare from beyond space and time that has been reawakened by global warming and toxic dumping, a nightmare the government tried to keep submerged. Neptune's Reckoning. Terror knows no depth

Bestselling collection

DEAD BAIT

A husband hell-bent on revenge hunts a Wereshark... A Russian mail order bride with a fishy secret... Crabs with a collective consciousness... A vampire who transforms into a Candiru... Zombie piranha...Bait that will have you crawling out of your skin and more. Drawing on horror, humor with a helping of dark fantasy and a touch of deviance, these 19 contemporary stories pay homage to the monsters that lurk in the murky waters of our imaginations. If you thought it was safe to go back in the water... Think Again!

@severedpress
/severedpress

Check out other great

Sea Monster Novels!

Matt James

SUB-ZERO

The only thing colder than the Antarctic air is the icy chill of death... Off the coast of McMurdo Station, in the frigid waters of the Southern Ocean, a new species of Antarctic octopus is unintentionally discovered. Specialists aboard a state-of-the-art DARPA research vessel aim to apply the animal's "sub-zero venom" to one of their projects: An experimental painkiller designed for soldiers on the front lines. All is going according to plan until the ship is caught in an intense storm. The retrofitted tanker is rocked, and the onboard laboratory is destroyed. Amid the chaos, the lead scientist is infected by a strange virus while conducting the specimen's dissection. The scientist didn't die in the accident. He changed.

Alister Hodge

THE CAVERN

When a sink hole opens up near the Australian outback town of Pintalba, it uncovers a pristine cave system. Sam joins an expedition to explore the subterranean passages as paramedic support, hoping to remain unneeded at base camp. But, when one of the cavers is injured, he must overcome paralysing claustrophobia to dive pitch-black waters and squeeze through the bowels of the earth. Soon he will find there are fates worse than being buried alive, for in the abandoned mines and caves beneath Pintalba, there are ravenous teeth in the dark. As a savage predator targets the group with hideous ferocity, Sam and his friends must fight for their lives if they are ever to see the sun again.

Check out other great

Sea Monster Novels!

Edward J. McFadden III

SHADOW OF THE ABYSS

Out of the past comes an immense horror. An ancient creature that must feed its voracious hunger.A massive landslide on Grand Bahama Bank sends a thirty-foot wave traveling at 150MPH toward the east coast of Florida, and the tsunami drags in something horrible from the depths of the Mid-Atlantic Ridge rift valley. Now a monster roams Florida's east coast and its shallows, searching for prey.Matthew "Splinter" Woods lives in Sailfish Haven. He's a washed-out Navy SEAL who lives off the grid on his dilapidated boat and has withdrawn from society rather than face his demons. But when his ex-girlfriend, charter boat captain Lenah Brisbee, comes to him for help, Splinter gets drawn into a battle that pits him against the strongest enemy he's ever faced as he races against time to find the monster before it turns the waters he loves blood red.

Eric S. Brown

PIRANHA

The rains came, flooding the sleepy, little town of Sylva. Sheriff Hanson never thought that he would be fighting a battle to survive against real life monsters. . .but with the waters came flesh eating, hungry creatures that swept through Sylva's streets like locusts, devouring everyone in their path.

www.ingramcontent.com/pod-product-compliance
Lightning Source LLC
Chambersburg PA
CBHW061241170626
46809CB00007B/2774

* 9 7 8 1 9 2 3 1 6 5 3 1 1 *